THE LENDERS

Also by Helen Christine

Full Disclosure

THE LENDERS

A Novel about Mortgage Fraud

HELEN CHRISTINE

Cover photo courtesy of timurok/iStockPhoto.com

Layout and cover by Gray Dog Press, Spokane, WA

THE LENDERS/Helen Christine – 1st ed. 2015

ISBN 978-0-9907222-2-9

Printed in the United States of America.

To my children and grandchildren.

ACKNOWLEDGMENTS

AFTER THE publication of my first novel, *Full Disclosure*, several people encouraged me in my writing, and I want to thank all of them.

I particularly thank the following:

Monica Edwards, Roxa Kreimeyer, Rosemary Stewart, Judy Bryant, Lillian Hegstad, Steve Wing, and Kevin Wing for promoting *Full Disclosure* on social media and telling others about it.

Julie Hart, for reading, suggesting helpful changes to my second novel, and encouraging me throughout the process .

Griffin Rain and Nancy Trevison, for reading, proofreading (more than once) and encouraging me to continue to tell my stories.

Russ Davis and Gray Dog Press, for editing, formatting, publishing, and supporting me on *The Lenders* novel.

Let's package the mortgages and
sell them to investors.

What could possibly go wrong?

CHAPTER 1

"They're making a movie, Mommy! They're making a movie!" the little boy yelled, excited to see the yellow tape police had put up surrounding a house and a car parked on the driveway next to it. "Can we go over and watch?"

"It's not a movie, Johnny. Those are *real* police cars and *real* policemen," his mother answered as she grasped the boy's hand and turned from their walk, retracing their steps to a home several doors down from the crime scene.

RUNNING ALONG the sidewalk in her new bargain-priced running shoes, Annie Robinson enjoyed the bright January morning in 2007, happy to have the sun shining instead of rain falling. She watched as the little boy and his mother entered a home. Concentrating on her run, she didn't spot the police cars immediately. When she saw them, she stopped and gawked at the surrounded house, police cars, yellow tape and officials methodically processing the scene. One of the detectives called for the entire street to be blocked off.

As a policeman approached Annie with the tape drawn to exclude her, she questioned him, "Hey, what's going on? Somebody get killed?"

"Can't tell you anything about it, Miss."

"Not even if somebody's dead?"

"Well, I guess I can tell you someone's dead."

"What happened?" she asked, expecting the policeman to tell her details of the death.

Instead, the policeman ignored her question and completed shutting down travel on the street, cutting off drivers who usually drove the street on their way to work in Seattle.

Disappointed at his rebuff, Annie did a U-turn, resumed her run on the sidewalk, and then decided to head back to her home.

Since she knew few of her neighbors and her house was half a mile from the crime scene, she thought it unlikely she'd known the dead person. The cop could have told me more, though, Annie thought to herself. Nothing ever goes on around here, and when it does, I like to know what happened.

Annie's four children expected their mother to start her day by running two miles through their neighborhood because that was often the only time she had to exercise. Thirteen-year-old Rachel made sure ten-year-old Gage got dressed in time to catch the bus, the six-year-old twins, Candy and Cammie, were fed and dressed for school, and Rachel herself was ready to be driven to school by her mother. When their dad, Brad Robinson, took a swing-shift job at Boeing, they'd all discussed how they'd distribute the early-morning chores to make the job hours work for them all. The reward for the children was a higher allowance made possible by the pay differential Brad would receive. The reward for Annie and Brad was a bigger paycheck and they hoped less strife in paying bills.

"You're early, Mom," Gage remarked as Annie shut the door after her return.

"Yeah, Mom," Candy agreed. "We're not dressed yet."

"I didn't run very far. One of the streets was closed down by the police. Yellow tape all around." Annie took off her running shoes. "The policeman told me someone had died."

"Really?" the three younger children chorused.

Rachel said, "Who?"

"I don't know. You know the neighborhood better than I do, Rachel." She described the house and told her which street had the yellow tape.

"It doesn't sound close to anyone I know," Rachel replied.

"No boys live there, I guess," Gage teased.

"Mom, make him be quiet," Rachel laughingly pleaded.

"Gage, be quiet." Annie grinned at them both and then clapped her hands and said, "Finish getting dressed, girls. And, Gage, eat the rest of your cereal. I'll take a quick shower, get dressed, and we'll be out the door in fifteen minutes."

By the time Annie got the three youngest children to the bus stop, Rachel to her school and then driven to her office in South Seattle, she had completely forgotten the crime scene she'd witnessed on her morning run. She began the second run of her day: Her work at Franklin Mortgage.

ANNIE WAS a senior loan processor at Franklin Mortgage where she was responsible for the quick documenting and verifying of information on Sherm Taylor's mortgage loans prior to sending the loan package to underwriting.

Sherm Taylor, a senior loan officer with Franklin Mortgage, had an "A" personality type and was sometimes over the top in voice volume. Loud and aggressive would often be applied to Sherm, but so would likeable and boy-like.

Whatever terms were used to describe Sherm, everyone at Franklin Mortgage knew he was a top producer and brought in more jumbo loans than any other loan officer at the company. In fact, he probably out-performed most loan officers in the Seattle area. About six months earlier, he had hired an additional loan processor to keep up with his volume of loans.

Annie Robinson got along well with Sherm. Often she could open a file, get necessary documents, obtain underwriting approval, and go to closing and funding within a week. None of the month-long time periods required by the majority of loan officers and their processors. Sherm liked her—she did her job well and that meant a shorter pipeline for his paycheck.

Annie didn't use any of Sherm's aggressiveness. Instead, the dark-eyed, curly-haired 35-year-old employed charm, coyness and her musical laugh to persuade their client's employers, bankers and others to return verifications to her promptly, as if there were urgency to their performance that meant so much to the entire world. Some called it "schmoozing." Annie called it getting her job done.

It bothered Annie that Sherm's new loan processor often seemed to be able to close loans even faster than she did.

"Have you got the insurance binder on the Butler loan? They're funding tomorrow," Sherm yelled at Annie.

"Called their agent ten minutes ago. I'll call again in five minutes if they haven't faxed it."

Sherm grunted assent.

Annie had enjoyed working on Nate and Judy Butler's

loan. He worked at an industrial plant and she worked at a bank. They had good and provable income and had saved a large down payment on the house being mortgaged. Everything was within underwriting guidelines so their loan had quickly been approved and the interest rate had been locked.

Neither Annie nor Sherm had any idea what they were asking from an insurance office when Annie called for a binder. All they expected was for someone to drop everything else that was going on and get them the paperwork that showed the mortgage lender's name on the loan.

Annie had been a loan processor so long she could remember when applications were thoroughly checked with an eye toward any number that would make an underwriter decline the loan and verifications took weeks as the applicants waited for approval. It was different now with loans requiring little or no documentation.

Annie's father and the company president were friends, and that friendship had helped her get the processing job at Franklin Mortgage. She had worked for Sherm about eight years. During that time she'd processed all kinds and sizes of loans ranging from conventional—those that were within the loan amounts eligible for purchase by the quasi-governmental agencies of Fannie Mae and Freddy Mac—and larger loans that were purchased by several investment banking companies. Sherm tried to specialize in loans of a million dollars or more to boost his fees.

"I'll be in talking to Carter," Sherm told Annie as he headed upstairs to the vice president's office.

It took three additional phone calls to get the insurance binder.

Later that day Annie learned it was Justin Diamond, a Franklin Mortgage accountant, who was the victim in the crime scene she'd seen on her run. Annie had known Justin much better than most Franklin employees and had often talked with him. She was surprised to learn he'd lived so close to her. The police were saying a gun had been fired by a drive-by shooter.

A drive-by shooter in their neighborhood? In the early morning? *I* don't think so, Annie said to herself. But who would murder him?

CHAPTER 2

A week after the death of Justin, Annie asked Sherm, "Are you going to Justin's funeral today? I want to if I can get everything done."

"Probably not, although I'd also like to go. I've got clients coming in," Sherm responded as he headed toward Carter Brislawn's office.

I liked Justin, Annie thought to herself. He didn't deserve to be shot and killed. I hope the police get busy and figure out who murdered him.

She worked through lunch and left at two o'clock for the funeral home. Her work was important to the people wanting to buy houses, and Annie felt she was making a difference in the world, but Justin's funeral was important, too.

SHERM TAYLOR walked as if he had bricks tied to the bottom of his size 14 shoes and approached everyone with the sound of clunk clunk instead of tap tap. When he entered Carter Brislawn's office, the vice president and assistant to the company president didn't look up before he said, "Hello, Sherm. What can I do for you?"

"Just wanted to let you know I'll have a record number of loan closings in the next few weeks. It's not as many as I had hoped, but the first quarter of 2007 isn't looking as positive as 2006. I've been getting a little push-back from some of the appraisers. Have you heard that from anyone else?" He sat down in the chair opposite Carter.

"Not much. The market's still going up and our profits are also." He closed the file in front of him and leaned back in his chair as he looked at Sherm, stroked his goatee, and continued, "We're having a terrific month."

"That's great. I must be imagining difficulties because I've had a couple good loans rejected. Or at least I've thought they were good." Then he changed the subject. "Justin Diamond's funeral is today. I'm not going but guess a lot of the office staff plan to go. Are you?"

Carter had a questioning look. "Who? Oh, yes, the accountant. No, I'm not attending." Then he said, "If you'll excuse me, I need to meet with Al," and he pushed his chair back. Carter took the cue and they both headed to the door. Carter's facial muscles hadn't moved during the entire meeting.

What a weird guy, Sherm thought as he walked to his office.

ALBERT PENDLETON, CEO and President of Franklin Mortgage, enjoyed being called "Al" and greeted all his employees with an outstretched right hand and a friendly smile. His small stature was not at all indicative of his powerful position after founding the mortgage company that now reached into three states.

Al enjoyed reading reports he received. How much money was the company making? How many mortgages were being generated? What was happening on the secondary market where their loans were repackaged and resold?

Carter often provided selected information for Al.

"Everything seems to be going well, Carter," Al said. "I'm pleased."

"Good," Carter answered. "I just saw Sherm Taylor and he expects to close millions in loans this month and most of them will go to Merrill Lynch." His expression told Al nothing.

Al buttoned his vest and jacket. "I'm leaving soon to pick up my wife to attend Justin Diamond's services. Are you going?" Al asked.

"No, I'm not," Carter replied without emotion.

Carter left after a few more questions and answers. Al hadn't learned anything from Carter's visit, and that was just the way Carter wanted it.

CARTER STOOD at his office window next to Al Pendleton's office and watched the ships in the harbor unloading and loading cargo heading in all directions out of Seattle. He'd grown up in a boat-loving family, a family that he abhorred thinking about, but this was a view he never grew tired of.

His thoughts weren't on the ships or his family, however. He stood contemplating his dislike of Al's management style, as he often did from this window following a meeting with him. Carter believed employees should be evaluated by their production results, results shown on profit and loss reports. It wasn't necessary to know the employees well.

On the other hand, Al Pendleton would visit with the men and women in his employ, chatting about their children and even their grandchildren in some cases. Carter thought these "chit-chats" were a waste of time that could be used in a more profitable way.

Al put people before profits. Carter put profits before people. It was a major difference between the two men.

And going to Justin Diamond's funeral? Carter couldn't imagine attending it.

CHAPTER 3

"Rachel! Get off your phone and help me. The potatoes need mashing and I'm making salad."

"But Mom, I'm talking to Scott!" Rachel yelled to her mother, not bothering to cup the mouthpiece.

"I don't really care who you're talking to. You've been on the phone for half an hour and it's time you got off and helped with dinner. Your grandparents will be here anytime and I'm not ready," Annie said with exasperation as she reached into the refrigerator for carrots to shred.

Just then the doorbell rang and Cammie ran to let Grandpa Andy and Grandma Linda Carmichael into the four-bedroom rented home that seemed to be exploding with activity. "How are you, little lady?" Grandpa Andy asked the twin daughter who greeted him with a hug.

"Just fine, Grandpa Andy. I got all A's on my report card. Candy got a B," she said proudly.

"I was sick when we had a test," Candy defended herself. "It wasn't fair."

"Well, I'm sure you'll do better next time, Sweetie," their grandmother chimed in. "You'll get all A's, too." She turned her head to Brad to greet him just as Candy stuck her tongue out at Cammie.

"Hi, Brad, how's it going?"

"Good, Linda. We've all made the adjustment to my new hours at Boeing."

Andy started visiting with his son-in-law and Linda went to the kitchen to mash potatoes since Rachel hadn't gotten off the phone.

"Thanks, Mom," Annie told her as she put the finishing touches on the salad and the food on the table. "Cammie, go upstairs and get your brother," she told the young girl.

"Gage, dinner's ready!" Cammie yelled loudly.

"Cammie, I could have done *that*!" Annie told her. "Now run upstairs and get your brother." She turned to her Peruvian-born, dark-eyed mother. "How did you manage to raise us kids and not go crazy yourself? Did we behave like these kids?"

"Pretty much," Linda replied with a smile. "We didn't have cell phones to contend with, though."

Annie laughed. "I'm glad to know our four aren't that unusual. I sometimes wonder."

The clatter on the stairs told the family that Gage and Cammie were heading to the table, with Taffy, Gage's dog, running behind them.

"She pushed me down the stairs," Gage complained as he fell into his chair.

"Did not," Cammie countered and smiled at her twin sister.

"Kids, that's enough," Brad told them in a raised voice.

Andy laughed at his grandchildren, but Brad and Annie had disapproving looks on their faces as food was passed around the table. Linda steered the conversation away from the children by asking Annie about work at her office.

"Just busy," Annie said as she helped herself to the potatoes. "There's hardly a free moment with all the refi's and home purchases. Sherm has two of us processing loans now." The pain she'd been having in her stomach returned and she brushed it aside.

Andy was putting a chicken thigh on his plate as he said, "When I was at the bank before I retired, we didn't approve all the loans I hear about these days. Of course, the way we did it years ago, before all the loans were sold to the big guys on Wall Street, was to keep the loans and service them ourselves. None of this slicing and dicing I hear about today just to make more money. We knew the people we made loans to. We really wanted them to own their homes, but we didn't want to lose money entrusted to us by our depositors so we kept a check on what was going on. Sometimes I get the feeling no one cares any more what's happening to the people getting the homes of their dreams. It's all about money and more money."

He looked at his son-in-law. "People like you and Annie have to compete with those who buy a house just so they can sell it in six months or a year to make a profit. And, of course, the bankers get fat fees every time the property's turned."

"We're getting ahead, Andy. We're saving so we'll be ready. It just takes time to find the right house at the right price," Brad answered.

"And housing prices just keep climbing," Annie continued. She'd heard her father's grumbling comments many times. "We thought we'd found one a couple months ago, but it was snatched out from under us. The people who bought it paid $10,000 more than the sellers were asking. I couldn't believe it."

"I think those buyers made a mistake," Andy replied. "I believe the housing market hit its high a few months ago."

Dinner was finished, the kids were excused, and the adults continued to talk about what was happening in the housing market in the Seattle area and in their lives.

Annie didn't contribute much to the conversation and her mind wandered. Her thoughts suddenly turned to

Justin Diamond. He'd seemed nervous when they'd last talked, and she'd sensed he had something he wanted to tell her but hesitated to say more. At the time she hadn't thought much about it, but since his death she'd wondered if he might have been afraid. She wished she'd asked him questions. It was too late now.

CHAPTER 4

Two weeks had passed since Justin Diamond's funeral, and the police didn't seem to have a lead in the case. There hadn't been a follow-up story in *The Seattle Times*.

No one in Annie's office had brought up his death either, and the mortgage loan process had gone on undisturbed. There were rumors that Franklin Mortgage might be sold to an investment bank, but so far they were unconfirmed by management. Annie thought a sale was highly unlikely because the company was a cash cow at this point. Why would Albert Pendleton want to sell?

Annie's intercom buzzed and the receptionist told her she had a visitor, Stephanie Diamond. Would she come out to the reception area?

Stephanie Diamond here? To see her? Annie didn't know Mrs. Diamond other than at her husband's funeral so she was puzzled as she walked to greet the accountant's widow. She took her hand and said, "Mrs. Diamond, how are you?"

"Please call me Stephanie. I'm still getting over the shock of losing Justin, but I'm doing better each day, thank you. Is there a place we can talk?"

Annie pointed to a small conference room off the reception area, followed Stephanie into the room and then closed the door. Just as she had at the funeral, Annie noticed how young Stephanie looked, a good ten years younger than the 45-year-old Justin. Stephanie's grief showed in her tired-looking eyes, but her firm shoulders and head held high expressed her determination to move her life forward even without Justin. Annie sat across from Stephanie at the small table.

Stephanie spoke first. "I'm sure you're wondering why I'm here. I wanted to come a week ago, but it was too difficult to talk about Justin's shooting and what he told me before he died."

Annie's puzzlement grew.

Stephanie continued, "I saw your name on the attendees register at Justin's funeral and I really appreciate your being there."

"He was well liked here at Franklin. I think quite a number of us were there."

"Yes. It was good of all of you to come. Even Mr. and Mrs. Pendleton came, and that pleased me very much." Stephanie hesitated a moment as if she didn't quite know how to tell Annie about Justin and then said, "Your name was the one that stood out for me, though, because before his death Justin told me about you. He said to contact you if something happened to him."

Annie was startled. "Why?" she asked. "I can't imagine what reason there would be to contact me. The police say it was a drive-by shooting, and I wouldn't know anything about that."

"I don't think he thought he'd be killed by a drive-by shooter, but for some reason he'd started to feel his life might be at risk."

Annie's mind was racing. "Why would his life be at risk?" Annie asked. "He wasn't doing anything at Franklin that people would be upset over, certainly not something in accounting." She shook her head. "I've doubted the police theory, but I don't think he was killed by anyone around here, and that's the only connection I had with Justin," she told Stephanie.

This time it was Stephanie shaking her head. "We've never had anything like this happen in our neighborhood— no drive-by shootings, ever. It just doesn't seem plausible to me."

Stephanie continued, "Justin told me people at Franklin Mortgage had been involved in committing fraud to get loans approved. He said he knew you didn't do that. You just bird-dogged and harassed people to get a file through underwriting." She laughed as she told Annie about Justin's comment. "He really admired you, Annie. Justin was always a very honest man, and it just doesn't seem possible he was involved in anything that would get him killed, but I'm thinking he must have been."

Stephanie produced a handkerchief from her purse and caught the tears starting to stream down her face, then blew her nose. "I want Justin's killer brought to justice, but if he was involved in something that would tarnish his memory, I don't want people to know and bringing in the police wouldn't protect him. Justin and I need your help, Annie. Would you try to figure out who might have had a reason to kill him? He knew about the fraud and maybe that's the reason."

Annie almost stammered as she replied, "I don't know what to say, Stephanie. I don't know how I can help. And I'm not aware of any fraud going on around here so Justin's wrong about that." It upset Annie to be told fraud could be occurring at Franklin, but she felt so sorry for Stephanie. She rose from her chair, put her arm around the distraught woman and softly said, "I have no idea what I can do but I'll think about Justin's words and try to figure out what he was talking about. Can I get your phone number, Stephanie? I'll call you when I know anything."

"*Please* call me when you learn anything, anything at all," Stephanie pleaded as she wrote down two numbers and then handed the slip to Annie. She had put "work" beside one number and "home" beside the other.

When Stephanie got up to leave, Annie gave her a brief hug.

I hardly know this woman, she thought as they left the conference room, but I think Stephanie Diamond has put my life on a new course. What could Justin have been doing before his death and why would he ask his wife to seek me out? I don't get it.

CHAPTER 5

Sherm Taylor hadn't given Justin Diamond a thought since the funeral.

As he drove to his sprawling home in Bellevue, he swore at the traffic getting on to the Lake Washington Bridge and then swore at the traffic exiting it. "Too many people moving to the Puget Sound area," he fumed, not thinking about the fact that the growth improved his business.

As he turned into his lengthy driveway, Sherm remembered he needed to write a couple of checks and get them in the mail the next morning. One was a check to his mortgage company and the other was on his boat loan. He ran his fingers through his neatly-trimmed blonde hair as he thought about the draw he'd received that day. The two bills came due just before his payday, and the habit of taking a draw provided enough money to see him through.

When his refinance mortgage was completed, he'd have sufficient cash to quit taking draws each month.

He pressed "open" on his garage door remote and drove the Mercedes in, next to his wife's Porsche and his son's BMW, and wondered where the car his daughter wanted would be parked. Well, he wouldn't worry about it now since at 15 she didn't have her driver's license. Maybe his 17-year-old son would be in college and out of the house by that time. He frowned. College would mean additional expenses and Lance had shown no sign of being able to get a scholarship, athletic or academic. Without letters of recommendation, he'd be lucky to get into any college with his abysmal grades and lack of interest in studying. Sherm had thought Lance would have a future in computers when he'd shown a strong interest in computer games as a youngster. But he hadn't gotten beyond playing games. The only thing he'd learned was a bit of geography as he learned where his opponents lived.

Sherm closed his car door and walked through the kitchen to the foyer and into the living room where Melanie Taylor, his wife of 19 years, sat on the large sofa, a drink on the end table next to her.

"Starting without me?" he asked as she reached for the glass. He walked to her and leaned over to kiss her cheek as the contents of the glass jiggled.

"You're late," Melanie said, bringing the glass to her lips.

"You're early," he responded as he walked to the liquor cabinet, grabbed a glass, put in ice and then poured Scotch over it. He sat across from her.

"Kids're gone?"

"Obviously."

"Bad day?"

Melanie stared at him and took another sip of Scotch. "Aren't they all?"

"I guess I was just hoping." He wondered exactly what he was hoping as he held his glass. That she'd keep sober? That she'd pay some attention to their kids? That she'd be at the door anxiously awaiting his arrival as she had when they first married?

They sat in silence. Sherm tried to start conversations about other subjects but got no response from Melanie as she finished her glass and then asked Sherm to fix her another.

"I think you should stop drinking," he told her. "You've had enough."

"I'll tell you when I've had enough!" she screamed at him as she tried to rise from the deep cushion. Her glass fell to the floor, breaking as it rolled from the area carpet to the hardwood lying beneath. "Now see what you made me do!" she accused her husband and lurched toward him.

Sherm grabbed her flaying arms, released her left arm, and slapped her cheek so hard he had to tighten his grip to keep her upright. Melanie glared at him and then passed out.

Sherm lifted her easily, carried her upstairs, and laid her on top of their bed. He straightened her legs before covering her with a nearby quilt. Then he retraced his steps to the living room and poured another Scotch.

The shattered glass and its spewed contents didn't catch his eye as he finished his drink and fixed another.

He needed to get Melanie to an alcohol treatment center, and to do that he needed money and her acquiescence. He rarely seemed to have enough money, though, and he never had her agreement.

CHAPTER 6

Brad woke Annie. "You're having another nightmare, honey," he told her as she tried to make sense of the disorder in her awakened mind.

Annie remembered her nightmare had had Justin in it, but that was about all she could conjure up from the quickly fading memory of her sleeping thoughts. It was always that way. By breakfast she never remembered anything about her dreams, other than that Justin had been in them.

Annie had told Brad about Stephanie's visit when she got home the evening following their talk. Brad seemed to think Justin's words had only indicated stress with his situation. He didn't believe it indicated murder. "And I don't think you should get involved," he had told her.

Annie wasn't so sure.

But she also wasn't sure what she'd be involved in. Murder? It didn't seem probable to her that Justin would have been purposely shot. Dishonesty at Franklin Mortgage? Impossible. Everyone at the company just seemed to be doing the job they were supposed to do.

The following week Annie tried to watch her co-workers more than usual. It was hard because she was always rushing to get her own work done, loans processed, and was always fighting the clock. Sherm didn't make it easy. Faster, faster, seemed to be his mantra. She was working as fast as she could, but his new processor, Angela, always seemed to get more loans closed than Annie did. *How did she do it?*

Franklin Mortgage had gotten into subprime mortgages, mortgages that didn't meet traditional underwriting standards and carried a higher interest rate the investment banks liked. In these loans, assets were marginal and income was sketchy. In fact, no-documentation loans were often used so little information given by the applicant was verified. It was a system of "trust me because I say so."

Annie thought this system was nuts. Her father did also. "These loan officers have every incentive to get people who want homes to buy ones they can't afford," he'd say to his daughter and anyone else who would listen. "Then it's up to the borrowers to make the payments they can't afford. Someday this is all going to come crashing down. Mark my words, the lenders and loan officers won't get hurt, but the borrowers will."

Stephanie called Annie on Friday. "Do you have any information for me?"

Annie felt she'd betrayed her when she said, "No. But I'm working on it. I'll figure out what Justin was talking about," she assured his widow.

Annie was stymied, though.

She brushed paper clippings from the copy machine table before pushing her documents through the machine. Why are people so careless about the workroom? she asked herself.

It didn't occur to her to look at the paper scraps to see what they were.

ANNIE RUSHED home to take Gage to his after-school soccer practice. She upset Rachel by telling her she was to stay with the twins and Taffy until they returned. "But I wanted to go to the mall with my friends." Rachel fussed.

"You can call them and tell them you'll meet them after dinner. And please get the potatoes peeled and put them in cold water. I'll be home in time to fry them and cook the meat. The sooner we eat, the sooner you'll be able to go to the mall." Rachel was still fuming when she called her friends.

Gage's soccer practice went well, and Annie enjoyed watching him play. When they got home, the twins and their sister were quietly playing a board game while Taffy watched and waited for Gage. Potatoes were covered with cold water.

"Good job, Rachel. Very nice, sweetie. And the twins behaved?"

"Yeah, when I said I'd pay them some of my allowance if they were quiet."

Both Cammie and Candy looked up and brightly smiled at their mother.

"You will *not!* Cammie, Candy, you're not going to get money for doing what you're supposed to be doing, and you were supposed to do your lessons and play quietly when you finished studying. Did you do your homework?"

Both girls shook their heads.

"Well, head upstairs and get it done. You have 30 minutes until dinner."

"Thirty minutes?" Rachel wailed. "But I wanted to go to the mall with my friends right away. Do I have to have dinner, Mom?"

"Yes. Your friends will still be your friends after dinner."

The following weekend passed quickly with Brad taking Gage to his soccer game and Annie taking the girls to their ballet lessons on Saturday. On Sunday they all went to church in the morning and in the afternoon the twins went to a friend's birthday party which necessitated quickly shopping for birthday gifts. By Sunday evening Annie felt as though she'd been running in a marathon since Friday afternoon. Actually, she thought she'd been running before that since work itself was a constant dash to the finish line.

Just before she fell asleep Sunday night she thought about Justin Diamond. She had neither the time nor the training to be a detective, she told herself. And at that moment she didn't have the energy either. Then she thought about Stephanie and the forlorn look on the widow's face when she'd visited Annie.

If something happened to Brad and she were in Stephanie's shoes, would everyone say they were too tired or didn't have time or didn't know what to do? *Would anyone help her?* She turned her head on the pillow. Tomorrow she'd focus on Justin's death. She didn't believe he'd been killed because of his work, but at least she'd try harder to find out.

CHAPTER 7

Al Pendleton teed off with a one iron on the third hole and watched the ball head into trees to the left of the green. He shook his head in disappointment and disbelief at his poor shot. His caddy took the club, walked with Al to the area where the golf ball had landed and soon found the errant missile. Al put it on the course and accepted the added point.

One of the foursome golfing that morning remarked, "You need more time to practice, Al. When you sell that profitable company of yours, you'll be able to golf more often with us. Get more practice time. Golf every day when the weather is as nice as it's been." He laughed. "My wife loves my golfing." He laughed again. "I thought I'd be bored when I quit working, but I haven't had any trouble keeping busy." He took a shot and his ball landed on the green about three yards from the hole. "See what I mean? It just keeps getting better."

Al grunted. He hadn't told anyone, other than his wife, about the prospective sale of Franklin Mortgage to a Wall Street investment company. The deal wasn't final yet, and until it was, he didn't talk about it, not even the possibility. He remembered what the World War II slogan was: Loose lips sink ships. He didn't intend to sink this ship because it carried gold.

It was time to sell and retire, though. Long gone were the days when he could write loan amounts, client names and details of his investment in a small notebook and carry it in his jacket pocket. He seldom told anyone how he had gotten started in the mortgage loan business. They'd think he'd been crazy. No credit checks, no property appraisals, no loan-to-value ratios. If the guy had a job and Al thought he'd make the payments on time, he got a loan. And Al carried the details in his pocket.

He and Gretchen incorporated their business as Franklin Mortgage, a name meant to convey honesty.

In the beginning the business had been slow to build. Al and Gretchen didn't have a lot of money to lend. But when payments came in and their funds grew, they grew the company and didn't spend the receipts. They lived on their income from his job as a wholesaler.

He went to night school and learned the banking business. And when Al and Gretchen thought they could manage without a paycheck, Al quit his day job. Al sold mortgage loans and Gretchen kept the books on them.

So many people wanted to buy houses and needed financial help that the Pendletons put a business plan together and hired employees to make everything work at an increased capacity. Al was a good salesman.

They were ready when they got an opportunity to sell loans to Fannie Mae and Freddy Mac. Securitization of loans made their business mushroom and profits grew exponentially.

"But I sometimes wish we were just starting out again, Gretchen," Al often lamented. "It was fun then. And I could trust a man's handshake. No one shook your right hand and at the same time took hold of your arm to show he was in control. It was just a handshake, and we had made a deal. Now I never know if I'm going to get kicked in the butt as I leave the room. It's a different world."

Claiming he had to get back to the office, Al left the group after nine holes.

He hadn't specified which office, and the one he went to in downtown Seattle was his CPA's. The Wall Street company, JWColbert, was well represented by their CPAs, attorneys and staff. Al thought Franklin Mortgage was well represented by his attorneys and CPAs in the room. When Al said Franklin Mortgage was a closely-held corporation, he meant it. He and Gretchen were the only shareholders.

The meeting agenda went beyond concepts of a possible purchase. Details were emerging. The purchaser wanted to look at the company books, and Al's accountants obliged.

Greed was palpable as monthly and yearly profit and loss figures were distributed following the signing of non-disclosure documents. Sheaves of mortgage loan details were presented.

No one from JWColbert seemed to see the real estate boom ending. The people in the room appeared to believe it would go on forever. And Al didn't tell them any different.

CHAPTER 8

On Monday morning, Annie had good intentions as she drove to work. She planned how she was going to help Stephanie figure out why Justin had thought Franklin Mortgage was involved in some kind of dishonest action.

She spent time slowly walking through the offices that she usually merely glanced at. The rows of loan processors, each with a computer and many files on the desk, didn't look any different from usual and were much like her own desk in a cubicle. So much was automated, but there still needed to be a paper trail that matched documents sent to closing and funding.

The loan officers and employees locking loan rates had offices surrounding the processing area, most of them fairly small but large enough to accommodate applicants seeking loans. The largest producers had more spacious surroundings.

A large copy room was at one end of the room.

Accounting, underwriting and due diligence were on the floor above the loan officers and processors, the same floor on which Al and Carter's offices were located.

She stopped at a couple of desks on her floor to visit but didn't stay long because she wasn't the only one trying to get work done. They were all busy.

Annie looked over at Angela Albright's desk and saw Sherm's other processor's eyes focus on her. Then Angela smiled. Annie walked to her desk and sat in the nearby chair. "I don't think we've had many chances to visit, have we," she remarked. "There's always too much to be done."

"It's difficult to keep on top of things," Angela said and pushed long blonde hair back behind her ear. "Sherm always wants things immediately." She covered up the file that was in front of her.

"Yes, he does," Annie replied and laughed, her dark ringlets bouncing as she moved her head. "Sooner if possible. You seem to keep up well, though, and get so many loans closed each month. I'm always impressed at how quickly you get documents prepared." She wanted to ask what her secret was but thought better of it. Angela wouldn't likely tell her. They were competitors in a sense.

After a few additional comments, Annie returned to her own desk. Angela smiled, Annie thought to herself as she sat down, but I didn't feel she wanted me anywhere near her work. As if I cared what she was working on.

When Sherm came in, Annie knocked on his office door and said, "It's me, Sherm." She resented having to ask before he said to come in. In seven and a half years working for him, she hadn't knocked prior to entering, but at the time he hired Angela he told the office, including Annie, that they shouldn't just walk in. Annie thought he was being either pig headed or big headed, but he was her boss so she always knocked.

"Come on in, Annie," Sherm responded and smiled as she did. "Sit down. How's it going today?"

"Fine. I haven't been here long." She took the chair Sherm had in front of his desk and then hesitated before launching into her inquiry. Sherm would probably be surprised. "I wanted to get your opinion on something," she began. "Before he died, Justin said there were dishonest people here at Franklin. He seemed very nervous. Do you know what he was talking about?" She shifted in her chair to get more comfortable. She felt Sherm was a good friend and would let her know if there were something happening in the company that validated Justin's concern.

To her surprise, Sherm became agitated. He pushed papers across his desk, as if in anger, and said, "Are you accusing me of something? Is that what you're doing? Well, I'll not stand by and be accused by a dead man." His voice thundered at her.

Annie was aghast. What made Sherm so angry? She hadn't accused him of anything. And neither had Justin. Sherm had taken her question very personally. Why?

She pushed back her chair and headed to the door. "I don't know why you're angry at me," she said. "I just repeated what Justin said. And he never accused you of anything." She looked back at him. "I thought if something were going on, you'd know what it was." She tried very hard to keep her temper, carefully shutting the door instead of slamming it.

She had deliberately not said anything about Stephanie's visit but instead had given Sherm the impression of a verbal comment to her. Maybe Stephanie wasn't reflecting Justin's paranoia. Maybe there really were illegal actions at the company. *Was Sherm involved in some shadiness?*

CHAPTER 9

During the week Carter Brislawn III stayed at his downtown Seattle condo. On weekends he often rode the ferry to his Bainbridge Island home and tried to catch an earlier ferry than the other commuters.

When he first bought his waterfront home on the prestigious island and was commuting, he'd stood on the upper deck to see the other ferries criss-crossing the Sound and watched for whale or other mammal sightings. Now he often stayed in his car for the journey or climbed out and briskly walked to the tables to read his business journals. He didn't need to listen to the loudspeaker to know when his ferry was near the island.

This Friday afternoon he waited longer than usual for the ferry walk-ons to exit the ship and tapped the steering wheel as he hummed along with the song playing on his radio. He felt good about the week just ended.

Franklin Mortgage had closed a record number of mortgage loans, and millions had been snapped up and packaged by Fannie Mae, Freddy Mac and Wall Street players. He looked forward to his paycheck. He'd also had other successes that week and he'd now be able to purchase one more large property.

The driveway to his home gently sloped toward the beach. When there was snow or ice, he cautiously inched his white Porsche down to his garage, but today he hardly slowed before entering the three-car cavern.

He tossed his keys on the table next to the door and called, "Rita, I'm home."

As he watched his girlfriend come from the living room, he thought again how beautiful she was. Dark brown hair, deep lavender eyes, long legs that seemed to stretch to the stars. Her arms reached around his neck and he drew her close to kiss her.

Together they walked to the credenza in the living room and he made both of them a drink before sitting on the floral couch, Rita next to him. He kissed her again and she smiled.

"Good to be home," he said.

"I'm glad you're here. Will you need to work this weekend, darling?" She buzzed his ear.

Carter smiled at her. "Only a little."

He slowly unzipped the back of her dress.

THAT EVENING as Carter sat at the grand piano and played Broadway show tunes for Rita, his eyes glanced at pictures of his parents displayed around the room. One in particular of his father always commanded his attention. Carter Brislawn II, a stern-looking man, was facing sideways rather than straight ahead, and Carter III imagined his father was looking at his son who was beyond the picture. Carter III never smiled at these moments.

The weekend was relaxing and the couple spent time on the large deck facing the water. In the early afternoons on Saturday and Sunday they sat on the beach and watched sea gulls, ships and sail boats as they sipped cocktails. Rita fixed breakfast and dinner and they snacked at lunchtime.

Carter commented to Rita, "I'm glad there are no children in our lives. I never want children. They complicate life, and I like my life the way it is." Rita didn't respond.

During the weekend Carter spent time on the Internet looking for properties in the Seattle area. If he thought Franklin Mortgage was involved in dishonest dealings, he didn't say anything to Rita and it didn't stop him from buying more properties.

Renting the houses he'd purchased had begun to take so much time that he had hired an agency to do that for him in spite of the cost involved. Having to talk with one person, his agent, was preferable to having to interview dozens of renters. Also, the properties had to be well groomed in the event he wanted to sell them, so he'd employed a maintenance company, saying, "I have no desire to mow a lawn." And, after purchasing his second house, he'd incorporated his business, with himself as the sole shareholder. He wanted to become a multi-millionaire and he was doing everything he could to reach that goal.

Monday morning he returned to his office. Rita stayed on Bainbridge. He looked forward to being with her again the following weekend, but in the meantime he had work and she had nothing to do with how he'd spend the week in Seattle.

It promised to be a good week.

CHAPTER 10

Friday afternoon had been an angry and stressful time for Annie when she saw Angela, Sherm's other loan processor, enter his office without the required knocking beforehand. Why didn't Angela need to announce herself? Had she forgotten? Coming so soon after her own difficulty with Sherm, she realized she was just being petty and tried to brush aside her negative feelings toward Angela, but, try as she might to find positive words, she finally admitted to herself that she just didn't like Sherm's newer hire. She was a fake. But how did she get loans closed so quickly?

Annie had spent more time than she had available that week trying to spot any dishonesty at Franklin. All she had found were more messes in the copy room. She brushed the scraps aside as she had done before and completed her own work.

The weekend was the only time Annie and Brad could go house hunting, so they set aside Sunday afternoon to drive around looking at "For Sale" signs, hoping they'd find one they could afford in an area south of Seattle. Brad's work would be close and Annie could manage the drive to her office. The children would have to transfer schools.

"Rachel, you'll need to look after the other kids while we look for a house," Brad told his daughter.

"But Dad," Rachel wailed, "I don't want to have to stay home and babysit. I have other plans."

"Change them," Brad said unsympathetically.

She continued her rant. "The twins are horrible and won't mind me."

Brad looked at Annie for help.

"Well, I guess we could take the twins, Brad. Cammie and Candy," she addressed the six-year olds, "run upstairs and get something to occupy yourselves in the car. Gage," she said as she turned to her son, "you can stay home if you want."

Rachel continued fussing. "Gage can't stay by himself so I have to stay home, too?" she asked.

Annie looked at Brad and then told the young rebel, "If you go out, you have to take Gage and Taffy with you and be sure they stay with you. And you're only to leave the house with friends who have a parent with them. Got it?" Her voice was exasperated.

Rachel read the sign. Her mother wouldn't budge from her position.

As the four of them got into the car, Annie said to Brad, "We do ask Rachel to take care of the kids a lot. I need to think of something special to do for her."

Three hours later Brad, Annie, Cammie and Candy returned from their search, tired and frustrated.

"We stayed home. Did you find a house?" Rachel asked.

"Yeah, did you?" Gage echoed.

"We found lots and lots and lots of houses. It was boring," Cammie replied and then announced, "I'm hungry. What's for dinner?"

"Mushrooms from the back yard," Annie told her, giving her the answer she and Brad often gave, reminding them all of the mushrooms a neighbor had once picked that turned out to create hallucinations and poisoned them. "Or we could have macaroni and cheese. Your choice." She looked at Brad. "Of course, you and I will have pork chops."

"*We* can't have pork chops?" Gage asked in a perplexed voice.

"You know Mom's kidding, Gage," Rachel responded. "I saw the pork chops in the refrigerator."

"But I'd like macaroni and cheese," the twins shouted in unison.

"Okay, okay, four of us will eat pork chops and two will have macaroni and cheese. Dinner's in 30 minutes," Annie said, relieved the twins would prefer the cheaper meal.

Later that evening after the children were in bed, Brad and Annie talked over the houses they'd seen. "Still too much money, Brad," Annie told her husband. "But I'm afraid if we don't buy one of them now, they'll cost more next month."

"Let's wait, honey. I have a feeling they'll come down in price soon."

Annie didn't know where he got that feeling. All she heard at work was that housing prices would only go higher.

On Monday the rush began again.

Late in the afternoon she called Stephanie, Justin's widow.

"I meant to call Friday but didn't have time."

"That's fine," Stephanie said. "I was rushing around also.

What have you found?"

"Not much really. Sherm, the loan officer I work for, is acting suspicious, but there's nothing I can put my finger on. He got angry when I suggested there might be something dishonest going on, but later he was fine. I'm sorry, Stephanie."

"Are you giving up?"

"No." Annie quickly responded. But did she believe there was anything she could find? She didn't know. "I'll keep trying to figure out what Justin meant. There must be something I'm not seeing."

"Thanks. You're my only hope," Stephanie said before hanging up.

Annie sat at her desk, wondering what she wasn't seeing as she watched Angela walk to the copy machine room with papers in her hands.

CHAPTER 11

In the middle of the week Carter got a phone call from his mother. "It's been so long since we've seen you. We're hoping you can join us this evening for dinner. In fact, dear, I won't take no for an answer. Seven o'clock?"

Having dinner with his parents was the last thing Carter wanted to do, but he'd learned years before that it was easier to agree with his mother than to disagree with her. "Seven o'clock will be fine, Mother."

"Then we'll see you. Your father and I will look forward to the evening with you."

Carter put the phone down gently. When he was younger, he'd slammed the phone when his mother finished a conversation, but at age 45 he'd learned it didn't make him feel any better. Nothing changed in their relationship, and he just tried to spend less time with his parents.

Their estate was on Mercer Island, reached by a long bridge crossing Lake Washington that bisected the Island on its way from Seattle to Bellevue. The shoreline home had been designed and constructed by Carter Brislawn, Carter III's grandfather, following his successful boat building enterprise in Seattle. Carter II had taken over the business following his father's death, and he and his wife, Claudine, now also claimed the large home which they had updated and remodeled.

Carter drove his Porsche along the circle driveway and parked in front of the brick house. He sat a moment contemplating the dreary evening and hoped it would turn out better than the last time he'd eaten dinner with his parents. He'd barely been able to check his temper and had hurriedly excused himself following the meal. He vowed he'd at least stay this evening for the traditional after-dinner cocktail.

The Brislawn butler opened the door for him since Carter had forgotten his key. Or perhaps he'd thrown it away. He wasn't sure. "Mr. and Mrs. Brislawn are in the living room, sir," the butler said and led Carter to them. Carter II rose from his chair as his son entered and shook his hand. Claudine waited until the younger Carter came to her and then leaned her head forward in anticipation of his light kiss on her forehead.

"We're so glad to see you, Carter," Claudine said. "We'd hoped you'd come by before now." She held a drink in her hand.

"Yes, son. Thought you might drop by. What are you drinking?"

"Scotch on the rocks."

"Good choice," his father said as he headed to the bar and poured his son's drink.

Claudine chatted on about nothing meaningful to Carter and at last they were called to dinner.

Carter wasn't surprised when his father brought up the subject of Carter's work. Obviously he hadn't learned from the previous visit that his son was happy with his job.

"Doing any interviewing with a bank or brokerage firm? They'd be smart to hire you, especially with your experience in the lending business." He looked at Claudine. "Your mother and I are still hoping you'll accept employment with one of the companies other Yale graduates have joined. Franklin Mortgage has been a good stepping stone for you, but we believe it's time to move on, or move up, so to speak." He took a bite of beef they had been served. "As you know, I could put you in contact with a few people."

Carter scrambled his food around his plate, as his mother looked disapprovingly at him. He knew this was a childhood habit he'd abandoned some time ago, but it kept returning whenever he was with his parents, especially Claudine. He put his fork down.

"But I like my job, Dad."

"Well, of course you do. Otherwise you wouldn't have stayed as long as you have. Your mother and I just believe you can improve yourself and make more money than you now make by joining a more prestigious company."

Carter knew his parents were very curious about his income, but neither of them would ask what it was and Carter would never tell them. It wasn't any of their business he felt. If they knew, they might feel differently about his work, but the disclosure wouldn't be worth it.

"I'll think about it," he replied.

Other than for his mother asking about any marital prospects, the conversation lapsed into more mundane subjects that all were comfortable with—the terrible state of the nation and the need to lower taxes. The housing market wasn't discussed, nor was Rita. He stayed for the after-dinner liqueur.

When Carter returned home, he poured another Scotch. Tomorrow he would get two appraisals on area homes and call his real estate salesman to sell one of his properties because the price had gone up so much since he bought it. He frowned that his father, and many others, would call it "flipping." He just called it a good business move and one that would make thousands of dollars for him.

CHAPTER 12

In the spring of 2007 Al and Gretchen Pendleton took Amtrak to New York City to see the bankers who were interested in buying their mortgage company. It took much longer than flying would, but Al wanted to get away from the office and believed this method of transportation would stifle the rumors about a prospective sale of the company. He told Carter he wanted a vacation and had never spent much time on a train.

"Gretchen is pretty excited about this trip," he said. "She's planning to shop and has some plays in mind."

Carter said, "No need to hurry. Take your time. We'll take care of business while you're gone. The loan officers are going full throttle and know their jobs."

Al thought the term "full throttle" was funny in view of their upcoming train experience and laughed. "So we'll all be going full throttle."

Carter looked at Al a minute before he got the joke. Then he laughed. "Yeah, I guess so."

After Carter left the office, Al filled his large briefcase with all the documents he thought he'd need for business discussions. On the way out he stopped at his secretary's desk and said, "Don't hesitate to call me if there's a problem. I'll want to know what's happening."

His secretary smiled back at him and said, "Have a good trip."

On Amtrak Al looked at the papers in his briefcase. He thought about the years when he'd spent time reviewing all the loans recorded in his notebook. This was a different analysis, but since he'd grown as the company did, he'd persistently looked through the company reports and statistics. He knew and understood them better than anyone else in the company. He also knew it was time to sell and retire. There were trends he wasn't happy about. He told Gretchen, "I can't keep my eyes on everything the branch managers are doing, and I don't trust all of them. Besides, the growth in real estate values won't go on forever, as so many in the industry believe, and I have the feeling we've reached the top of this huge real estate boom."

Gretchen didn't read through the reports, but Al apprised her of them and she agreed with his timing. She wanted to sell.

"We'll have time to do whatever we want, dear. I've been looking at a map of all the train routes in the United States, and I think we'd love to travel this way," Gretchen said.

"You mean 'ride the rails'?"

Gretchen laughed. "Yes, I guess I do."

The New York meetings went well. Al's attorneys and accountants had flown in to attend them and then flown back to Seattle again after all the parties had signed papers agreeing to the sale of Franklin Mortgage.

Later Al shook his head when he and Gretchen discussed the agreed-upon price for the purchase. "I can't believe what they agreed to, but the sale is valid. I feel we sold a gravy train at just the right time, dear, since sell high is the proverbial advice and I think we're at the top of the market. Quality control is down and delinquencies are up." Gretchen nodded her head as he commented further. "I hear loan officers complain that if we don't lower standards at Franklin Mortgage, they can't compete with other lenders. But I also see competition bringing about more loan defaults because borrowers, who were stretched to meet income qualifications, now can't meet their obligations. If JWColbert had looked at the figures we provided and checked out the loans, they would have seen that. We shouldn't need to babysit their analysts."

"How did you ever come up with 'gravy train,' Al? I think the sale must be providential," Gretchen told him.

They returned to Seattle by plane.

Chapter 13

Al had asked for 24 hours before the sale would be disclosed to the media, and he felt fortunate there hadn't been a leak of the news. Government regulators had been apprised, but their silence had been expected. He wanted to tell his employees before they got it second-hand.

Before calling department heads together in the conference room and arranging for simultaneous conference calls to the other branches, Al had told Carter Brislawn about the sale.

"You what?" responded an incredulous Carter. "Without even talking to me about it?"

"What would you have said if I'd talked to you?"

Carter stammered a reply, "Well, I'd have, I would have given you a hundred reasons *not* to sell, one of which would be the tremendous profit Franklin Mortgage has been generating. Another would be that sales are up and still climbing. A third would be that our loan officers are furiously competing in this market, both in the subprime area and in jumbo loans. It's all going great. Why sell *now?*" he asked.

"For the three reasons you just gave me. It's a tremendous time to sell a profitable mortgage lender. Why wait until the market starts coming down?"

"I think it will keep going up for some time. We're not close to a high."

"Maybe you're right. We'll see. But the deal's done, Carter."

"I think you're making a big mistake." A furious Carter pounded Al's desk with his fist and left the room, slamming the door behind him.

Al shrugged his shoulders. Carter's response had been expected. He hoped others in the company would see it more like he and Gretchen did.

When he explained that their jobs were intact and the business would operate as it had under his ownership, the assembled management personnel asked questions but seemed to accept the change. Most of them were more interested in their pay checks than in who owned the company. Maybe they'd get increases since the new owners had massive amounts of capital, or so they thought. Bonuses would likely be larger. It would probably end up being a good change for them.

When the news hit the floors of the loan processors and other support personnel, their questions were pretty much the same as upper management's had been. How would the ownership change affect them? And the reply was that there would be no change. They'd do their work as they had before, and perhaps they'd even see more money in their checks.

AN ANGRY Carter attended the management meeting led by Al and said all the proper things about the sale.

Nothing would change, Al had said. But he hadn't said that Carter would now be president of the mortgage company, and that had been Carter's goal during the years of his apprenticeship, years when he had stepped in to do Al's work when Al was gone. Would the new owner, overloaded with personnel they'd want to promote, move Carter to a lower notch in their organizational chart?

Carter had been counting on Al's retiring and putting him in charge of Franklin Mortgage. That's what should have happened.

A SHOCKED Annie could scarcely believe the company had been sold. She'd read about the buyer, JWColbert, but it was just another Wall Street company to her. Her job wouldn't change, she'd been assured, and that's all she wanted to hear. She needed this job and the bonuses she got.

No dishonesty had come to her attention at the company, and she had begun to think Justin had been wrong. Any purchaser of Franklin Mortgage would certainly have looked into loans generated and possible fraud. They'd have been stupid not to. It didn't occur to her that greed could mask all kinds of problems, especially if blind eyes produced more cash for a buyer.

Annie called Stephanie and told her she hadn't found anything substantiating Justin's thoughts. "Franklin Mortgage has been purchased by JWColbert. I don't think they would have put money down for a company whose loans weren't good ones. I think Justin was probably killed by a drive-by shooter, like the police decided, Stephanie. I'm sorry to disappoint you."

When she hung up the phone, Annie had a sinking feeling in her chest, as though she'd given up on something important.

CHAPTER 14

JWColbert made its presence known immediately by sending personnel from New York to Seattle, and each day a change was made with signs, stationery or documents, indicating the new ownership name, Franklin Mortgage, a JWColbert company. It wasn't the first time JWColbert had visited the Seattle office, but it was the first time employees were aware of their presence.

True to Carter's predictions, JWColbert brought in additional personnel to oversee some departments such as due diligence and accounting. However, much to Carter's surprise and also his pleasure, they asked him to assume the presidency.

"There's no one with the knowledge you have, Carter. We feel you're the best person we can have in this most important role. We have all the confidence in the world in you."

His new title included a large jump in compensation, and Carter didn't hesitate to accept JWColbert's offer.

The Seattle Times' front page story pleased Carter. It recited Franklin Mortgage's history under the ownership of Al Pendleton, its growth through the years, and its new owner's confidence in Carter Brislawn III as company president. It even quoted JWColbert as expressing their belief that Brislawn was the best person they could have in this most important role because of the immense knowledge he had of the lending business. The *Wall Street Journal's* story quoted extensively from *The Seattle Times* and carried the same picture.

Right after the newspapers ran their stories, Carter II called his son, "Congratulations, son. Just read about you in the *Journal*. Your mother and I are very proud of you. Can you come for dinner this week?"

Dinner with his parents was at the bottom of his to-do list and he didn't want to bring it any closer to the top. He pled extreme pressure at work. "I have mountains of papers on my desk, Dad, and not enough time to get through them. Sorry I can't make it this week."

"Next week?"

"I'll try, but I'll just have to see. I want this new position to work out for me."

Carter II said he understood and hung up the phone while shaking his head. "I'm sorry, Claudine."

Carter III wasn't sorry. He intended to work through the week and spend the weekend on Bainbridge Island with Rita.

CHAPTER 15

Sherm was elated at the news of the company's sale once he determined their due diligence wasn't going to be sharpened. His closings had bumped up with the addition of Angela's work. It didn't bother him that much of the underwriting was being done by automation; in fact, it helped him since he'd figured out how to make the automation work for him instead of against him.

He was also starting to get closer to Carter. And since Carter was now president of Franklin Mortgage, Sherm thought he had an edge whenever there was a question about a loan. Carter's motto seemed to be "sell, close," exactly the same as Sherm's. Sell the loan. Close the loan. Make more money.

But even though he made more money, there was never enough. The boat, the house, the vacation home, the kids. By some miracle Lance had gotten into college. The miracle of a scholarship hadn't happened, however, so the cost had to be borne by Sherm. Out-of-state tuition to the institution that had accepted his son was a major new expense, one that both he and Melanie had agreed to take on. Although Melanie hadn't done much to make the expense easier to bear, Sherm was happy to have his son gone from the house, and out of state was a bonus. He felt Lance's drive was one step above that of a slug.

Sometimes he regretted his feelings toward Lance, but these were times when his pay check and production bonus were particularly large. When he felt strapped, as he did this day, he reverted to blaming everyone in the family for how expensive their lives were.

Today was the day to blame Madison, his daughter.

Prior to her getting a driver's license, he'd given in to purchasing a new red BMW for her. A week after obtaining a permit to legally drive the car with one of her parents, she sped, alone, down the two-lane road leading to the Taylor' driveway and failed to see a pedestrian crossing the road until it was too late to stop. She bumped and knocked the woman down.

Fortunately for Madison and the pedestrian, the woman wasn't seriously injured. However, Madison was already known for her fast driving while unlicensed, and the woman and her husband felt Madison's wealthy parents would be amenable to a financial settlement in lieu of a lawsuit and the subsequent negative publicity.

They were correct.

The second mortgage on their home had been funded that day. Sherm had tried every other means to get the settlement money, but in the end a second on their beach-front home had been the cheapest and easiest solution.

When Sherm arrived home, Melanie was already drinking. It was only the middle of the afternoon.

"I'm bored," she lamented as she took a sip of the martini she'd fixed herself. "Madison and I both are. We've decided it would be a good idea for us to take a vacation trip to New York City. Do some shopping. See a few shows. She's been so stressed out over the accident that she's not been herself. Don't you think a trip would be good for her?" She took another sip.

A trip to New York? Melanie and Madison had done that before, and Sherm was still getting over the sticker shock from their visit.

"We can't afford a trip like your last one," he replied, "and you drank all the time."

"Did Madison tell you that?" his wife pouted, looking at him with her large eyes and long lashes.

"She didn't have to. The hotel called and told me about the damage you'd done to the suite."

"Oh, they didn't either! We left the hotel room exactly as we'd found it, all neat and tidy except for the beds. We even wiped up around the wash basins," Melanie said defensively.

"Of course you did." Sherm's voice was starting to rise. "Just as you keep everything around here 'neat and tidy.' That's why our maid is always wanting a raise because you're always tidying up the place so she won't have anything to do." He headed to the wet bar to fix his drink. Wednesday or not, he intended to enjoy a few cocktails.

The next morning Sherm's head seemed to be exploding as he drove to his Seattle office. Staying home hadn't been an option because, as usual, he had loans in process that needed his hand.

Annie had been watching for him and knocked on his door when he arrived. Sherm wanted to say 'stay out' instead of 'come in,' but it was Annie and he rarely denied her entrance.

"I need to talk with you about the Cramer loan, Sherm," she began. "They're nice people, but I can't get the numbers to work out so they qualify for a loan. Their income just isn't enough for the house they're buying. I know it's a small loan, but they need at least another five hundred a month income. Is there something I'm not seeing about the file?"

"I thought the numbers worked out just fine," Sherm answered. His head was bursting. Why of all days was this the day Annie had decided to work on the Cramer file? He wished he hadn't given it to her.

Annie held the file in her hand as Sherm said, "Give me the file and I'll give it to Angela. She can make the numbers work, I'm sure."

Annie looked flabbergasted as she handed the Cramer file to Sherm. Why had he given it to her, he asked himself.

CHAPTER 16

Annie's day had started out so well. She'd been able to run while Rachel helped get the other kids ready, and everyone had gotten to the bus, school or work when they were supposed to. And then Sherm whiplashed her. She was stunned. A loan officer giving one of her processing files to another processor had never happened to her in her long history of working in the mortgage business. She'd gotten files from other processors, but never the reverse. Devastated, she just sat at her desk as she watched Angela make her way to Sherm's office.

Annie had spent more time than usual trying to juggle the numbers to make them fit into the parameters underwriting would permit. She had met the Cramers, a young couple trying to buy their first home, but no matter what she did, the borrowers didn't qualify. They didn't have enough income.

Angela would quickly find this out and she'd have to tell Sherm to tell the borrowers. The Cramers would be upset, but Annie told herself it probably would be good in the long run because they'd soon get behind in their mortgage payments and could lose the house they'd invested in. The borrowers should find another house they could afford, in her opinion.

The incident hurt Annie, though. Sherm had handled it poorly. Annie had worked for him long enough to know that he reacted very quickly to news he didn't like, and she'd just dropped it on him, so she had handled it badly also. He'd probably apologize to her when Angela couldn't get their income to work.

The experience was still in the back of her mind the following weekend. Brad asked what was troubling her, and she told him the story. Shrugging his shoulders, he dismissed the incident with the comment, "Women get upset over nothing. You should forget it."

Now Annie was furious with two men.

Weekends lapsed into familiar ruts with activities of her children, and once again the two days disappeared almost as quickly as morning fog.

Annie still kept busy at work, but she noticed the piles of files on her desk awaiting processing were shrinking. When she passed Angela's desk, the file load seemed to be growing. Annie had fewer loan closings than usual. She couldn't see how many Angela had, but she had the feeling the newer processor was gaining on her. It was such a puzzle, but she could tell Sherm was asking more of Angela and less of her. Why?

THE ESCROW company Sherm liked to use was located a short distance from the Franklin office. Clients signed closing documents in that office and usually Annie had no need to visit because the file had been processed and underwritten.

When Annie came to the escrow office one morning, she was bringing the original insurance binder for a file. It was a pretty day and she hadn't been able to run as she liked to, so she saw it as an opportunity to get exercise.

She was well acquainted with most of the escrow closers and greeted the receptionist, Brenda. "Good morning. I got the original binder for the Samuelson's loan. Would you put it in the file, please? They're supposed to close tomorrow."

"Sure, Annie. Be glad to."

Annie looked up from Brenda to see Mr. and Mrs. Cramer exit Teresa Wright's door, with Teresa, an escrow closer, following them. "It's nice to have met you folks," Teresa said to them, and then saw Annie and said, "Nice to see you, too, Annie."

The Cramers remembered Annie and greeted her. "We've missed talking to you, Annie. Angela has been fine to work with, but we loved your sparkling laugh."

A surprised Annie responded from habit. "I've missed you also. I hope everything is fine."

"Oh yes!" they both exclaimed. "We love the house and plan to move in right away," Mrs. Cramer said. "Teresa told us the loan should fund the end of the week."

"I'm happy for you," Annie replied as the Cramers left the office.

Stunned, Annie turned to Teresa. "I didn't think they qualified for the house they wanted. I couldn't get the income numbers to work out. What happened?"

"The file came through with underwriting approval so they must have shown enough income to Angela and Sherm. I have no idea what happened."

After Annie left, she wished she'd asked Teresa to show her the file. But then she thought again. Teresa would wonder what was going on that Angela finished the processing, and Annie was still smarting over Sherm's handling of the file.

Something had happened, though, something having to do with the numbers provided by the Cramers. She thought of Justin. Was this what he was talking about?

GOING THROUGH a garbage can is yucky, Annie thought to herself as she used a term her twins would use. Chewing gum was the worst thing because Angela didn't wrap it in paper before tossing it in the can. And she chewed a lot of gum.

Discarded papers were squashed in a ball before discarding, and Annie wondered if Angela had played basketball when she was young. She would have been very good, judging by the number of squashed balls inside the garbage can.

Annie had tried to think of every way she could to see what Angela was up to before trying this method. But each night Angela carefully cleaned off her desk, putting files in her desk drawers, and then locking them. She was much more thorough about this than Annie was. Annie never locked anything but tried to remember to put files in drawers. Often she didn't even do that because, she reasoned, she'd just need to get them out the next day to work on them. Who would care?

Too many days had passed since the Cramer documents were finalized so Annie didn't think she'd find anything in Angela's garbage to link her to changes in the Cramer's income. Something else might have been "tossed," though, that would be a clue to what was going on. Maybe she'd find a method Angela used to get faster closings. So she kept working around the chewing gum and other nasties in spite of her disgust.

With half the garbage spread on the floor in front of her, she reached in for a fairly clean wadded-up paper and got her first clue, and it was a big one: an original document signed by borrowers with white-out on the income shown. Angela or someone else had actually blotted out what the borrowers had written! Annie sat stunned. She couldn't believe her eyes. A second later she furiously started pulling out other trash and found another document that appeared to be altered.

Now she knew how Angela had become such a productive processor. If the evidence didn't work, she'd change the evidence.

Quickly Annie went through the remaining garbage. She unwadded what looked like a signed document on which white-out had been used on an asset the borrowers listed. Again, if the evidence didn't work, Angela changed the evidence. Magic, a la Angela.

Annie checked her watch and hurried to reload the basket with the garbage she'd strewn about her. The cleaning crew would be arriving soon and Annie didn't want them seeing her.

She drove home with thoughts so glued to her discovery that she almost drove past her own house.

She'd left her children with Rachel in charge after the younger three had gone to bed. Rachel had been given strict orders to let no one into their home and she had complied with her mother's commands before going to bed.

Annie unlocked the door and quietly stood alone in the living room. Then she went to the kitchen, opened the refrigerator door and took out a piece of cheese to put on a cracker. All the while her mind was jetting from one thought to another. Was Sherm telling Angela to make changes? How many files had she changed? What other changes had she made? Were other processors doing the same thing? Were other loan officers involved? Was Annie the only one in the office who was processing loans the "old-fashioned" way?

She walked back into the living room, turned on a table lamp and sat munching her cheese and cracker, mulling over her discoveries. She thought about the discarded paper scraps she kept finding in the copy room. It hadn't occurred to her that these were evidence of document changes, but then she'd not really looked at the papers before putting them in the trash to tidy up the room. She still didn't know, but it seemed likely to her now. Loan processors would need to make a copy of the changed document and make it look like an original so they could put it in the file for loan approval.

Annie felt stupid not to have realized before this evening what was going on at Franklin. So much for being honest, she said to herself. Keeping your nose to the grindstone and all that, she thought. Trying every way to make numbers work to get borrowers into the houses they wanted. Rush, rush, rush. Worry, worry, worry.

And all she had needed to do was load up on white-out.

Exhausted at last, Annie took a shower, went to bed and didn't wake up when Brad came home.

CHAPTER 17

When JWColbert bought Franklin Mortgage, not only was Carter fearful about his job, but he also wondered if the new owners would exercise stronger due diligence. Would they look more sharply at the mortgages they'd be approving before sending them to the secondary market for resale? Would they exercise greater care?

It didn't take long for him to realize their due diligence was practically non-existent. They focused their concern on how many mortgages were approved and how many dollars were involved. Were profits going up? That was what they cared about and the answer was *yes*.

When Al Franklin was heading up the company, Carter always needed to be cautious about his activities. He never knew for sure what Al knew about his vice president. That concern no longer existed, and after the initial months following the transfer of ownership, Carter led the company in the manner he wanted.

And he bought more houses, sometimes keeping them longer than six months, the maximum time "flippers" usually liked. If the value had gone up as much as he desired, he sold. However, if he anticipated more profit, he held on. He told himself he could be patient.

Patience had been necessary in his youth. How he disliked his childhood. He remembered the stress trying to excel in matters he didn't care about, all to please his father.

"I want you at the plant tomorrow," Carter II had said in a voice that wouldn't condone the answer his twelve-year-old son wanted to give. "We're performing a process you need to know about."

Carter III couldn't have cared less about building boats.

Young Carter knew boat building wasn't the career he wanted. He didn't like the plant, the heat, the workers. But his father always insisted his son would grow up to delight in all of it, so rammed company knowledge into Carter much as the completed boat would be rammed into water.

The one thing young Carter liked about the business was the accounting, seeing the costs to build boats and comparing them to the sales price when they were completed. Could they build boats for less money? How?

Carter II had been trained the way he wanted to train his son. See what happens in the plant. See what actually goes on. Experience it all. Learn by doing.

Carter III wanted to learn by the numbers.

The conflict ruled their lives.

ANNIE'S VISIT was unexpected, but it didn't perturb Carter. She excitedly told him about her discoveries and waited for his response.

"I finally figured out how Angela has gotten so many loans closed in such a short time," she began breathlessly. "She changes the numbers on documents so they work out. She uses white-out on the original documents!"

Carter had looked up from papers on his desk after Annie opened the office door. He welcomed her with a "good to see you, Annie," comment. He knew that was a stretch. He just wanted the employees to work at their jobs. He was never particularly pleased to see them in his office. Loan processors' names were on his financial reports, and, since Annie was working for Sherm, the most productive loan officer, Carter was familiar with her and her work. He'd visited with her only a couple of times, though.

"That's quite a claim you're making. Are you sure?" he replied to her excited accusations against Angela.

"Yes, I'm sure. I spent quite some time going through her garbage to find the evidence."

Carter smiled and raised his eyebrow. "You went through her garbage?"

"Yes, and it was nasty. I've never seen so much chewing gum. But it was worth it because the altered documents were there."

Carter looked down at his desk a moment and then lifted his head before replying. "Do you have the documents with you?"

Annie handed a file folder to him. "Right here, the ones I found. You can see the alterations."

Carter opened the file and took a few seconds to look at the papers before closing the manila folder. "I'm not sure these are valid, Annie. They could have been documents the borrowers later changed and then re-signed before underwriting approval and escrow closing. Angela could have merely been showing what changes were later made. We really have no way of knowing, do we."

It was a statement, not a question. And Carter left no opportunity for Annie to object before he continued.

"Of course, you are competitors in a way. Perhaps you desire to see something dishonest in her work."

As he watched Annie leave his office, he wondered if it had been a mistake to point out Annie might be jealous of Angela.

But he really didn't care what Annie thought so long as she processed Sherm's loans. And Carter didn't care what Angela was doing, or Sherm for that matter. Sherm's production was all that mattered, and Sherm could do anything he wanted to keep the numbers going up. Selling boats or selling mortgages, the bottom line was all that mattered.

Carter saw his personal fortune growing through his job and through his real estate. He was nearing his goal of becoming richer than his father. He smiled with pleasure.

Chapter 18

Annie was furious with Carter and threw the file with the alterations on her desk. She'd gone to him because she didn't want to talk to Sherm again, not after his anger the last time she'd mentioned there might be dishonesty in the company. This time she had proof, and the only question in her mind was what Sherm knew about it. Was he asking Angela to make changes? Of course he was, she thought.

She'd talked with the president of Franklin Mortgage. There was no one with more authority than he had, and he'd dismissed her charges. Annie couldn't figure out what more she could do. Except to quit her job. Quit her job? She couldn't. Her family was depending on her income.

As Annie thought about Angela and her "magic," she realized she hadn't had stomach aches since discovering the source of the magic. Fraud was still occurring, but white-out had cured her pains.

WHILE ANNIE had been watching Angela and trying to discover how she processed loans so quickly, another woman had been transferred to the Seattle office from JWColbert in New York. The quiet and discreet presence of Monica Sullivan went unnoticed by most employees of Franklin Mortgage.

Carter had been told by JWColbert that Monica's job was to see what improvements could be made in the Seattle operation. Since she didn't appear to be in contention for Carter's job, he paid little attention to her following their initial meeting. If there could be improvements at Franklin Mortgage that would produce better profits, he was all for her finding them.

What Carter was not aware of was that Monica Sullivan's expertise was in due diligence and fraud detection.

Her supervisors at JWColbert had asked Monica to put together a cohesive plan for better oversight of their recently purchased company after they found rapid growth of the mortgage lending company had resulted in a patchwork system of communication. There was a due diligence department, but it was ineffective. When Al Franklin had been there, he'd known everyone in all the offices. He'd known what everyone was doing. He'd made a point to know. The notebook method of tracking lending data had served him well. With him gone, a system was needed and more accountability was essential. "You're to get a handle on this," they told Monica.

She had a small desk in a small cubicle in the large loan processing area. Her view of the processors blocked the view of the harbor they could see, and Monica didn't mind at all. The busy copy room held her attention.

CHAPTER 19

Sherm Taylor approached Annie's desk as she looked up to see him. Sherm had talked a lot to himself after Annie's last visit, and he'd finally decided he needed to tell her he felt bad about his behavior. Feeling bad didn't totally describe his feelings, though. He worried she might discover how much he was involved in changing loan papers.

He sat in the chair next to her desk and confessed, "Annie, I'm sorry. I behaved badly when you came to see me with your concerns. I shouldn't have gotten angry with you, and I don't know why I did. Just a lot of pressure, I guess. Anyway, I hope you'll forget about the incident."

Annie nodded her head and answered, "Of course, Sherm. I understand."

Sherm didn't know what else to say. The short reply wasn't what he'd expected. He had thought she would repeat all the claims Justin had made, and Sherm was prepared to nod his head as though he agreed or make a few "yes" or "yeah" comments. Her silence confused him.

When she said nothing more, he handed her another file to process and get to escrow. "One week?" he suggested.

"I'll do the best I can."

When he got up to leave, he told her "thanks."

Women are so difficult, he said to himself as he walked back to his office. A guy never knows how they're going to behave. I thought Annie would yell at me, or argue with me, but she just sat there. Well, I apologized and that's going to be it for me.

Sherm sat in his office only a few minutes before he went up to Carter's office. His heavy footsteps alerted Carter to Sherm's presence and he closed the file in front of him as he said, "Hi, Sherm. What can I do for you?"

"Just checking in. Anything new going on that I should know about? I mean anything new JWColbert is working on?" Sherm took a chair opposite Carter's desk. "I've heard they sent someone from New York to try to make us more efficient. The redhead in the corner cubicle. She's going to have to get around more if she's trying to figure out where we can improve. I didn't even see her for quite awhile." He grinned at Carter.

Carter smiled back at him. "I believe she's there just so we cross our T's and dot our I's. Window dressing of a sort. New York isn't looking for more efficiency. They think they bought a cash cow, and they're right. We're doing a good job for them."

"I'm having a great month, just like last month. Angela's working out well." He waited to see if Carter told him Annie had complained about Angela. Carter didn't say a word about either of them.

They visited a few minutes before Sherm left, feeling confident that Carter would be in his corner if Annie started making waves.

Sherm felt good. His paychecks were growing and bonuses just kept coming as he closed more loans, being careful to give Annie only the applications that fit squarely within lending guidelines. He had gotten caught up on his debts, even pre-paying his son's college expenses.

He had started doing more advertising for clients and was finding everyone believed it was time to buy a home or refinance the one they had. No documentation loans and five-year balloon payments were easy to sell because no one believed there would be an end to the skyward reach of home values. In five years, his clients could expect to refinance at lower rates than they were getting on their current mortgages.

Doubt about his future forecast never entered Sherm's mind.

He knew the loans he made were being sold into the secondary mortgage market and he was unconcerned. It was all good. Everybody was making money as Sherm originated mortgages, JWColbert packaged and sold them, and investors purchased them, often having insurance that had become part of the process.

Each month he challenged himself to sell more mortgage loans. He'd reached the point where the object of the loans had changed from being for the benefit of the clients and now was for his own benefit.

Sherm left the office and felt so good that he whistled as he drove his car down his driveway. It had been such a good day, and it seemed to him that Melanie was drinking less after she and Madison returned home from their New York City trip. Madison reported to him that her mother was "relatively" sober during the visit.

"Let's do dinner out, Babe," Sherm said as he walked into the living room. "I feel good. Feel like celebrating with you, the most beautiful wife a guy could have. What do ya say?" he asked Melanie as he walked to the bar at the end of the room and poured his Scotch. He looked at the liquor bottles and decided his wife hadn't started drinking but a short time earlier. It was a good sign.

Melanie rose from the large couch, walked over to Sherm, and kissed him. "I like that idea, sweetheart.

Somewhere romantic. It's time we treated ourselves." She handed her glass to Sherm. "Would you freshen my drink please, darling?"

Sherm did as requested. "We could get a room at that hotel you like. Maybe order dinner in. What do you think?" He followed her to the couch.

"I think that would be lovely," Melanie responded.

The Scotch went down easy. Life is good, he thought to himself as he called for reservations and then a limousine while Melanie packed overnight bags for them. No sense bothering to drive when they could leave the driving to someone else and arrive in a limousine.

The liquor and money flowed. Yes, life was good.

CHAPTER 20

That same weekend Annie continued to stew over the office happenings and her conversation with Carter. She didn't feel defeated, but she definitely felt like she'd been kicked in the stomach. And she hadn't sensed the kick was coming. She'd thought she'd be supported in her discovery.

She had decided Justin Diamond was wrong about her co-workers, and now, when she'd found he was correct, she wondered if he'd also been right to suspect something might happen to him. But Annie kept denying such a possibility.

Soccer and ballet occupied the family on Saturday. On Sunday they went to her parents for dinner. The twins and Gage immediately brought out the games Grandpa Andy and Brad always engaged them in, while Rachel continued to talk on her cell phone.

"I'm sorry, Mom," Annie told her mother as they worked together in the kitchen. "I'm always on her to get off the phone, but she doesn't listen to me."

"It's okay, honey. Let's hope she'll grow out of it and be a member of the family again soon. I recall the battles we had with you on a variety of issues, and you turned out pretty good. Just keep working with her."

Linda brought out lettuce, tomatoes, green onions and other salad ingredients and asked Annie to chop them for the salad. Then she mixed the dressing. "I notice you seem preoccupied, though. Is there something else on your mind? The kids' school work? Your work?" She slid the ham back into the oven and set the timer for another ten minutes.

Before answering, Annie started cutting up the tomatoes and cucumbers to put with the lettuce. "Oh, I don't know, Mom. I guess work is work the world over. There are probably problems in everyone's job." She opened the can of olives. "I'm just tired of mortgage lending and some of the things I see. No one cares *how* loans are approved these days, just so they go through the pipeline and are approved and closed. And everyone gets paid," she added.

Linda turned her head to look at her daughter. She'd never heard Annie express herself like this. "Have you talked with your dad? He might be helpful." She checked on the green beans on the stove. "Years of his work at the bank might give you some insight into your work."

Annie didn't answer. But she didn't discount his help either and decided to talk with him after dinner.

She suggested that her father take a walk with her after dinner and Linda asked Brad to help her with repairing a broken switch Andy hadn't gotten around to fixing.

Andy chatted amiably as they followed the sidewalk through the neighborhood. Then he asked, "Okay, so what do you want to talk to me about?"

Annie laughed. "Am I that transparent?"

"Well, today you are. You've been pretty quiet, and you don't often suggest a walk with me after eating. So I figured you had something on your mind. What is it?"

"Stuff at work, Dad. Things that I've found out about."

"Like what?"

"Like using white-out to change documents clients sign."

"*What?*" Andy almost shouted the word.

"I'm not kidding, Dad. I've found signed documents that have been changed so everything is within underwriting guidelines."

"You must be mistaken. That's fraud!"

"I know."

Andy didn't say anything for a minute as they walked and then said, "Who's doing this?"

"It's Sherm's other processor, the one I told you about. She got a loan processed and closed that I knew the borrowers didn't qualify for. I'd worked the figures myself and the nice couple were about five hundred dollars short on their income for the house they wanted to buy. They were in the escrow office when I happened to go there, and the escrow officer said everything in the paperwork was good and underwriting had approved the loan. I just couldn't believe it." She remembered how she'd felt when the borrowers greeted her. She remembered the pit in her stomach. "One night when everyone was gone I went through Angela's garbage and found other papers she'd changed."

Andy stopped walking. "You went through her garbage?"

"Yes, and it was yucky!"

Andy roared his laughter. "I can't believe you actually went through her garbage." he said as he continued laughing.

"Chewing gum! Wads of chewing gum. She balled up each and every paper she discarded, including the chewed gum. I think she must chew a pack every day. I took a shower when I got home."

Andy was bending over by now, unable to control his laugh. Annie started to laugh also and they both just looked at each other trying to stop.

"Oh, Dad," Annie finally said. "You've always been able to make me feel better, just like I do now."

"Good, honey. I'm glad you do. But this is serious business. You don't change signed documents." Andy and Annie started walking again. "Have you told Sherm?" And then before Annie could answer, he said, "You wouldn't need to, would you, because he already knows."

"Yes, he would be the one to ask her to make the changes."

"What about Mr. Brislawn? Have you said anything to him?"

Annie told her dad about that unhappy experience, including his comment that she might be jealous of Angela. "I felt like I was in junior high school and was being scolded by the principal."

They'd reached Andy's house when Annie asked, "Would you please not say anything to Mom or Brad? I don't want Mom worrying about me, and Brad has just brushed my concerns away. I'll tell him when I think it's a good time."

Andy agreed and said he'd think about a solution other than contacting authorities. "I'm proud of you, Annie, and that you're not a part of this deception."

Somehow she felt better just knowing her father's reaction. He hadn't doubted any part of her story.

It was only later that she wished she'd told him about Justin.

CHAPTER 21

Carter had taken the ferry to his home on Bainbridge Island on an August Friday, having declined his parents' invitation to dinner during the week.

His father had called to congratulate him on a short article in *The Seattle Times*:

> *Franklin Mortgage announced today loan volume has continued to increase since its acquisition by JW Colbert, a New York investment company, exceeding expectations by analysts. The Seattle-based company under the presidency of Carter Brislawn III has recently opened a new office in Vancouver, Washington, employing twenty staff.*

"Your mother and I are very proud of you, Son," Carter II had said, "and we'd really appreciate your coming."

"Thanks, Dad. I'm glad you called, but I'm afraid I can't make it this week. I'm checking on some real estate and will be out of town. Another time?"

"Yes, yes, whenever you can come. We'll be glad to see you."

Carter had hung up with no regret.

The last phone call before he left the office had been from his property appraiser who continued to please him with increased values on the properties Carter purchased. "Are you sensing any downturn in the market?" he'd asked the young man and had been happy with his response. Carter's portfolio was worth millions. The debt

Carter had picked up in order to buy the real estate was manageable with the income he received from Franklin Mortgage.

Buying real estate had become addictive for Carter. He wanted more and more and more.

The ferry cut through the smooth waters of Elliot Bay as Carter watched from the bow instead of staying in his Porsche, drawn by the lovely sunset he'd seen from the dock. He'd recently purchased a painting of the Bay the artist might have rendered from the same spot on which Carter stood. They both probably thought Puget Sound held beauty the world hadn't fully appreciated. Carter hoped the world would never know.

When he reached his beach house, Carter briefly regretted Rita wouldn't be there. Then he told himself he didn't need her complicating his life.

The last he'd seen her had been shortly after the news that Franklin had been bought by JWColbert and he'd gone to Bainbridge, still angry about Al's betrayal, as he called it. His frustration had been intensified when he thought how his father would browbeat him over a probable demotion. In his imagination he heard his father's voice reacting to the news that someone else had become president of the mortgage branch of the Wall Street company.

"What? You didn't get the job? Well, I'm not surprised. I've said all along either you should have come aboard my company or taken a position in banking and investing. You've been wasting your time working for Al Pendleton."

The more he'd thought about it, the angrier he'd become.

When he'd walked into his beach home that Friday evening, Rita had greeted him with a kiss. "I have your drink prepared and dinner will be ready in half an hour, sweetheart. We're having chicken in wine, potatoes au gratin, and asparagus spears, with crème brulee for dessert. Sound good?" she'd asked.

He'd answered "yes," but when she'd served dinner, he'd eaten sparingly. Instead, he'd filled up on liqueurs following the meal.

As they'd enjoyed the weekend walking on the beach, sitting in front of the fireplace, making love, he'd continued to drink and to nurse his anger, saying nothing to Rita about the company sale. By Sunday morning he was scarcely speaking about anything at all.

Rita completely misread his silence.

"It's so lovely here, Carter. I'd like to stay forever," she'd begun and leaned over to kiss him as they sat together on the couch. "I have the feeling you want me to marry you and you're not sure I'll accept if you ask me."

"Really?" he'd answered and then said, "And I suppose you'd like to get married to me?"

"Yes, I would. Wouldn't you like me to be your wife, sweetheart?" she'd replied, expecting a return kiss.

Carter had stared at her, amazed at her impertinence. "You're out of your everloving mind, if you think I'm going to get married." he'd responded. And then he'd hit her, and hit her again and again until she had fallen from the couch into a heap on the floor.

She had wept and said, "But, but I don't understand, Carter."

Without hesitation, Carter had said, "Of course you don't. You don't know me." His face had reddened as he continued, "You don't want me, you want my money and the things I can buy for you. You want to tell me what to do and what not to do. Well, I don't want to be told by you or anyone else. Get it?" He'd gotten up from the couch and walked to the bar to mix another drink, taking a long sip before putting the glass down.

Rita had stared at him in shock, then gotten up, walked haltingly to the bedroom and bathroom where she'd packed her belongings, and then she'd left the house in her Miata.

Carter hadn't talked with her since.

This evening, once the sun went down, a chill set in and Carter built a fire in the large stone living room fireplace prior to getting something to eat. He'd stopped for eggs and bread before catching the ferry and quickly scrambled three eggs and toasted two pieces of the wheat bread, then covered the toast with butter and marmalade from the refrigerator. He sat in front of the fireplace while he ate. He'd gotten used to Rita being with him on the Island, and he thought about her. It would take a little time to get her out of his head, he told himself. But he had no intention of changing his life by getting married. Marriage would only mean someone trying to tell him what to do.

After fixing a drink, he played Cole Porter songs on his piano, sipping the Scotch between tunes. He hummed *You'd Be So Easy to Love* and then abruptly got up from the piano, slammed his father's picture across the room, and sat again in front of the fireplace, his legs stretched out before him. When his glass emptied, he got up, fixed two more drinks, lay on the couch and fell asleep.

He woke to rain on the roof and a cold fireplace. Grumpily he got the fire burning again and made coffee, glad to find the coffee beans but irritated with the need to grind them. The odor of brewing coffee brightened him a little. With his filled cup in his hand, he again perched on the couch, then got up to turn on his iPod set in its dock. Beethoven filled the room.

He watched the rain.

Mid-morning he realized he needed to eat and again fixed scrambled eggs and toast, this time putting raspberry jam on the toast. He felt slightly stiff from sleeping on the couch.

At noon he reached for his briefcase and took out the contents which he'd intended to get at earlier. Sheaves of paper held all his real estate transactions over the years and he spread them on the cleared table in front of him. Addresses, appraisals, debts owed by the sellers, prices paid, debts owed by him, and, on properties he'd sold, the prices he'd received. His Boardwalk of properties. Then he looked at his bank account numbers.

He spent time on his computer working on additional analyses while a variety of music sounded from his Bose speakers. He banked up the fire he'd made to keep out the chill. The rain continued.

The following day he looked at paperwork he'd brought showing production at Franklin Mortgage. Everything was going smoothly. Loans were being produced and immediately sold into the secondary market. It didn't bother him that loans they produced were later sliced up and put into a variety of portfolios. He briefly wondered how anyone would ever track an individual loan, but he assumed it was being done by the Wall Street people who were being paid millions.

What he wasn't looking forward to in the coming week were the meetings in New York City. He'd assumed on his first visit to the JWColbert office after his appointment as president of Franklin Mortgage that he'd be treated with deference. Instead he'd had little opportunity to express an opinion beyond the spreadsheets in front of him. Each visit to the New York office reminded him of visits with his parents.

A looming melt-down of the entire operation never occurred to him.

CHAPTER 22

For the first time since Justin's death Annie ran past his house on her early-morning exercise routine and noted the living room window coverings were closed. Probably Stephanie got up later than she did, Annie noted, since she had no children requiring additional time before she drove to work. Annie looked at the driveway where Justin had been killed and could almost see him that fateful morning, unaware he would be dead in a few violent minutes. The neighbor's driveway almost abutted the Diamond cement and only a thin strip of grass separated the two properties.

Annie stopped and took a better look at the two garages and their driveways. The drive-by shooter could have shot the neighbor if he or she had happened to be leaving the house when the gunman passed. If it were a drive-by shooting.

Annie hadn't talked to Stephanie for weeks and told herself she hadn't called because of her busy schedule, or lack of a schedule at times. The discovery of fraud at her company and Carter's failure to support her findings had devastated and depressed her much more than she admitted.

Stephanie was still on her mind when Annie reached her office so she picked up the phone, dialed the work number Stephanie had given Annie, and called, hoping the woman would answer so Annie wouldn't need to wait for someone to summon her.

Stephanie's voice responded to the ring, "Hello, Woodbridge Elementary. This is Stephanie. May I help you?"

Annie was startled to learn Stephanie worked in the office of her twins' and son's school. On their infrequent conversations it hadn't occurred to her to ask where she worked.

"Hi, Stephanie. This is Annie, Annie Robinson. I didn't know you worked at Woodbridge. How are you?"

"Fine, Annie. And I'm glad you called because I planned to call you to see if you could come to my home and visit."

Annie didn't hesitate. "How about tomorrow, early evening. Would 6:30 interfere with your dinner?"

"Not at all. I'll plan to see you," Stephanie replied and they both hung up.

So not only was Stephanie a neighbor, she worked in the office of the school her children attended. She hoped they weren't regularly sitting in front of the principal's office. She hoped they minded their teachers.

So much for hopes. She needed to get to work.

The office looked the same as it had the previous Friday, but Annie saw it differently on Monday, and she looked at her co-workers with suspicion. They all smiled at her as they passed by her cubicle, and she smiled back, but everything had changed and she didn't trust the faces they displayed.

Several times she visited the copy room to try to see anything remiss, and she wasn't disappointed. The processors were hardly trying to disguise their handiwork as they cut and pasted figures or signatures.

She felt stupid. She felt nauseous.

At one point as she was about to leave the room, one of the loan officers came through the door, looked around, and then casually cut off the signature on a document, glued it to another paper, and as a final touch made a copy of the changed document before leaving. The scrap of paper he had trimmed was still near the cutting board, and Annie quickly retrieved it. The loan officer had performed "Angela magic" on an unknowing borrower.

The loan officer had worked for Franklin Mortgage almost as long as Annie had and she knew him well, but he had been so intent on his changes that he hadn't even seen her. He'd committed fraud right in front of her.

Wasn't fraud something you had to look hard to discover? Something so well hidden that almost no one would be able to detect it? Annie had always had that impression. It had to be committed by a mastermind, didn't it? Yet that loan officer is no mastermind, Annie said to herself. He really isn't terribly bright and in any other market he wouldn't have closed so many loans. But in this market he'd succeeded. Now she knew how. It was magic.

As she left the workroom, the new woman at the company came in and said, "Hello. I don't believe we've met. I'm Monica Sullivan." She smiled as she greeted Annie.

Annie smiled back and said, "I'm Annie Robinson, and I'm a processor for Sherm Taylor. Are you a processor?"

Monica's smile made Annie suspicious. Her new discovery no longer permitted someone to smile and not have her wonder if it was real. What was the woman up to?

"I'm from the New York office and have been trying to find ways to make communication better within Franklin Mortgage since it's grown so much," Monica explained. "Lots of times as companies get larger, it's necessary to streamline." She seemed to be analyzing Annie as she talked. "You've been here a long time so perhaps you have helpful ideas."

Annie shook her head. "No, I don't think I can be very helpful. I just do my job and don't know a whole lot about the company. Sherm keeps me busy."

How did Monica know she'd been with Franklin a long time? Had she been snooping? What else did she know? Did she suspect Annie of fraud just because everyone else seemed to be dishonest? Annie didn't believe Monica's cover story. What was she *really* doing at Franklin Mortgage?

Irritated by her findings of co-workers changing documents and by Monica asking questions she didn't want to answer, Annie left the room and walked straight to her desk where she put the incriminating signature scrap in the file. Since no one except her father believed her story, it probably wasn't necessary to keep this new evidence, but it wouldn't hurt either.

Sherm was late coming to work and quickly shut his door when he arrived. Good. Annie didn't want to talk with him.

At 11:30 she went to the lunchroom and cooked her Top Raman noodles in the microwave, then ate lunch at her desk instead of staying in the lunchroom where she usually ate with others at the company. She didn't want to see any of them. Without her, she told herself, they could sit around the tables and talk about how they were cheating the world. And how much their bonuses would be. And how great their jobs were and how they were helping people. Yeah, helping people get into houses they couldn't afford.

By the time Sherm called to tell her he'd locked a loan, she'd worked herself up so much that she almost told him to drop dead. But she didn't. She thought about her own paycheck and told him she'd get right at the closing papers.

So much for being above the others, she thought.

After dinner on Tuesday, Annie asked Rachel to take care of her sisters and brother and left Stephanie's home phone number with her. The drive took no more than five minutes.

Stephanie greeted Annie enthusiastically, as though they were long-time friends, and Annie returned her large smile.

"You have so much energy," said Annie. "Four children wear me out. How do you deal with so many all day and then still have energy in the evening?"

"I love my work and truly enjoy the youngsters. Maybe I wouldn't feel the same way if I worked at a junior or senior high school. They have bigger problems I think."

Annie hesitated to ask but decided she had to find out. "Do you know my son and twin girls?" What if Stephanie said "yes" because they were always sitting in front of the principal's office?

"Yes, I know who they are, but I don't know them well since they never cause problems. You know how it is— the difficult kids are the ones everyone knows." Stephanie smiled at Annie as she responded to her question.

Annie could have hugged her hostess. Brad and she always had had good conferences with all their children's teachers, but their behavior at home often made Annie doubt everything said at the conferences. Well, she was a believer now. "Thank you, Stephanie." She didn't say anything further about her children. Why spoil a good moment?

They sat in the living room of the ranch-style home. Stephanie served coffee and brownies and Annie wondered if they were Justin's favorites. "These are very good," she told her hostess. "Homemade?"

"Yes. I enjoy cooking and baking. I've gotten so I'm much better than I was at cooking for one person, but it's impossible to bake for just one so I take treats to school a lot. They always seem to disappear. Before Justin died, they never lasted long, but now…," she paused and then said, "I imagine you do a lot of cooking."

"As little as I can get by with actually. But everyone's always hungry so I've gotten pretty good at quick meals. My folks often invite us to dinner on the weekend. I try to get my daughter Rachel interested, but right now all she's interested in are her friends and talking with them on the phone. It drives me crazy."

Stephanie laughed.

Annie was surprised how comfortable she was with Stephanie.

"I know you called me, Annie, but I had planned to talk to you about something I've found out about Justin's death," Stephanie said. "So I'm glad you could come here. I don't know if you noticed our neighbor's house, the one to the right of us and adjacent to our driveway."

Annie nodded.

"Justin and I didn't know the family well before he died. About all the conversations we'd had were 'hello' and 'how are you,' that sort of thing because they're Hispanic and we don't speak Spanish and they, at least the parents, don't speak much English. They seemed nice, but we just hadn't put ourselves out to be friends. I've told myself that it was because we were so busy, which is the truth, but I wish I'd done more now."

She put her cup down and continued. "I was outside on Saturday working in the yard and one of the boys came over. I was startled because he's never come into our yard before. In fact, I've hardly seen the children, all except the youngest who is still in elementary school, Woodbridge. The teenager came over and introduced himself. Said his name is Antonio Perez and asked me to visit his parents in their home."

Annie wondered where this story was leading. Why would she be invited into the neighbor's home after all this time?

"Of course, I followed him next door and found his parents, Jose and Maria Perez, were waiting for me to come. They were very hospitable and insisted I have a cup of coffee and some pastries she'd made. Antonio, who asked me to call him Tony, said he wanted to translate because Jose and Maria were concerned their English wasn't good enough for me to understand. And I think they wanted to be sure I understood why they hadn't said anything to the police when Justin was shot."

Annie put her cup down just as she had started to raise it to her lips.

Stephanie stopped her story for a minute and took a sip of coffee. Then she looked out the front window as she said, "It's so hard for illegals to talk to the police. They live in the shadows as much as possible, always fearful they'll be returned to their homeland. They depend on their children to speak for them."

Suddenly Annie understood. "They told you they'd seen something but wouldn't tell the police because they feared being deported!" she exclaimed.

"Yes," Stephanie said in a quiet voice. "Their fright wouldn't let them say anything to the police when they knocked on the door. Tony had spoken for them and told the officers his parents were in bed at the time of the shooting and no one in the house had been aware anything had happened."

"What did they see? Did they hear the shot?" Annie excitedly asked, having a hard time waiting for Stephanie to tell the story.

"They saw someone talking with Justin."

"*What?* A drive-by shooter doesn't stop and visit with his victim."

"It wasn't a drive-by shooter." Stephanie's voice was exasperated. "Jose saw Justin and whoever it was with him from the living room window and thought it strange they'd be visiting in the driveway at that time of the morning, but he left the window and went into the kitchen. It was a few minutes later that Jose heard the shots. He ran back to the window, but saw only a car driving away from the curb and Justin on the pavement."

"He should have told the police," Annie angrily said as her jaw jutted out.

"Jose knows that. He kept apologizing over and over to me. And I guess I understand, though it's hard to find out after all this time that Justin was deliberately shot and his killer got away." Stephanie was shaking her head in disbelief. "In some ways, I'm glad to know it wasn't a random kind of thing, but on the other hand it's hard to deal with the idea that someone shot him on purpose."

"Jose should have told the police what he saw." Annie couldn't keep anger from her voice. "He let a killer get away." She got up from her comfortable chair and walked to the front window to look at the street in front of Stephanie's home, all the time thinking how Jose had let Stephanie and Justin down. "Even if he talked to the police now, it's been too long for them to track down whoever had been visiting with Justin. Far too long. Did he describe the man?" she asked as she turned.

"Not well. He had a jacket on. Dark hair. Slim. Maybe six feet tall. Jose isn't sure," Stephanie said, frowning as she gave Jose's imprecise description of the killer.

"Not very helpful. Eliminates blond, fat, short killers, and that's about it."

Stephanie laughed lightly. Annie saw an aching heart.

After a minute standing by the window, Annie went back to her chair, puzzled by the quandary they faced. "What do we do with this new information? Can we go to the police with it?"

Stephanie didn't hesitate before saying, "No. That would probably make life even more difficult for Jose and Maria. They're so frightened about being deported, and I just can't be instrumental in that happening to them. I just can't," she almost seemed to apologize as she lowered her head for a second and then continued. "We've got to figure something else out, catch the killer some other way."

"But how? And who?" Annie felt helpless and slightly disgusted with both Jose and Stephanie. She wasn't a detective and the biggest lead she had she couldn't use because they didn't want her to. Did they think she could pull a rabbit out of a hat?

She said goodbye to Stephanie and drove home.

On her short drive, though, Annie realized that the reluctant Jose had tardily established one important fact: It wasn't a random shooting by an unknown drive-by shooter. It was a murder committed by someone Justin knew.

CHAPTER 23

Carter Brislawn never squirmed. Sitting at a table in a conference room at JWColbert's New York office, he rarely talked with the men who sat next to him either. He was interested in what was being said by the chairman and wanted to know what was happening within the company, but that was the extent of his listening. He watched others, their expressions, body language and any fidgeting, believing their outward appearances and tone said more than their actual words.

That knowledge was the one thing he credited to his father. And the belief had served him well.

Carter never heard negative reports from a corporate officer. Always positive, the chairman expressed optimism about the economy, company growth, and improving sales. Carter detected no sign of internal problems in his body language this morning.

Most of the attendees were sales-oriented personnel and branch managers from areas around the United States.

JWColbert was in the process of acquiring another mortgage lender, Gilbert Lending, based in Texas, whose book of business was substantially the same as Franklin Mortgage. Jumbo to subprime mortgages, with high-end borrowers seeking to buy-up or refinance homes, on down to low-end, barely-able-to-qualify first-time homebuyers, and everything in between. If someone wanted a home loan, Gilbert Lending said "Come see us!"

It was the kind of company JWColbert wanted to own, the cash-cow kind.

Carter paid attention to the discussion about Gilbert Lending because he thought he might glean helpful information about their operation. But he didn't. It was built solidly along the lines of the business model of Franklin, and, from the conversation he heard, the company seemed to be doing precisely what Franklin was doing so well.

One of the participants at the table, a member of the due diligence committee usually attending the same meetings Carter did, brought up a discussion of more "problem" loans in the Gilbert Lending portfolios than he'd seen in others.

"I don't like some of what I see," he commented. "I know housing prices have gone up, but the percentage of growth is wacky, from my point of view. Are we sure of these figures? And the income of borrowers? They say they're making 'X' amount of dollars, but I'm not sure they are, and we have no verification. If they tank, we're stuck."

Carter heard grumbling around the table, and the man next to Carter said in a low voice, "There goes due diligence again, popping all the balloons just as the party starts." He folded his arms.

Carter looked around the table and saw the same expression as his neighbor had on almost everyone else's face. And many of them sat with their arms folded. Carter folded his, too.

The chairman proceeded. "Yes, that's why it's important to get loans into the secondary market right away, not that I think they'll 'tank,' as you put it, but because we can't afford to hold them long. We need to re-sell them. As you know, that's how the market works. And with so many loans being packaged and sold together, there's very little risk for an investor. They expect a few bad loans in a portfolio, and they have them quantified as to overall risk by the rating agencies, AA on down, so they know what they're buying. Any other comments?" He didn't wait for any before moving on.

Carter rarely visited with any of the participants, preferring to spend his time reading through reports.

On this trip Carter spent a little more time in New York than he usually did. One day he went up to Yale in New Haven, Connecticut, to look at the campus and visit with professors he'd enjoyed. They remembered him and were glad to see him and were happy to hear how well he was doing.

Money and prestige were great drugs. Carter enjoyed the feeling of success.

CHAPTER 24

"Hey, I hear JWColbert bought another lender," Sherm announced as he walked through Carter's door. He seated himself across from Carter as Carter closed up the open files on his desk. "I've heard of Gilbert Lending— out of Texas, right?"

"Yes, about our size, I believe, doing the same kinds of loans we do," said Carter. "It should be a good acquisition. JWColbert thinks it'll make the kind of money we're making for them." He didn't say anything about the comment made by the due diligence person at the meeting he'd attended. "You're not having any problem with loan quality, are you?"

"No, no. Everything's good." Sherm speculated whether Carter was aware of all the changed documentation going on at the company. Probably. It would be hard for him to miss seeing something. On the other hand, Sherm rarely saw Carter or any other management personnel on the processing floor. Well, Sherm certainly wasn't going to say anything and he knew no other loan officer would. Al Pendleton may have started to figure it out and that's why he sold. Sherm didn't know and didn't care. He believed Carter Brislawn only wanted the numbers to look good.

Sherm still thought Carter was strange, but Carter's personality didn't bother him and he kept visiting his office to uncover any information he could.

After Sherm left Carter's office that morning and returned to his own office, he spent time looking over loan applications that had been signed. He put them into two piles, one for Annie and one for Angela. Angela received a couple more files than Annie, who received only those applications that fit squarely within underwriting parameters.

Sherm had started giving seminars for people interested in buying a house or refinancing their homes and had a Power Point presentation developed, very nicely done with technical enhancements including Flash visuals. In the presentation he briefly talked about the secondary market, but the prospective borrowers were interested only in what they saw affecting their own needs. What did it take to get loan approval? How much could they get?

With his income growing, he also had money to hire a marketing specialist, Brian Duke. Brian had put the successful seminar together.

"Don't put in too much about ratios, Brian," Sherm had instructed him. "Just the bare essentials and don't get technical. Give it lots of glitz and make everyone aware that I'm the best person to get advice from without my having to say it to them."

The purpose of the seminars was to get borrowers to come to Sherm as an expert. And with Brian's help, Sherm succeeded.

Sherm carried the two piles to his two processors and plunked them on their desks, staying briefly to go over the contents of a few of them. Angela greeted him warmly, but Annie was still angry and hardly said a word to him.

Well, so much for that conversation, he said to himself as he left Annie's cubicle. I really don't care if she's angry as long as she does her work as well as ever. But he missed her cheerful disposition he'd grown so used to over the many years they'd worked together, and he wished he'd hear her sparkly laughter.

CHAPTER 25

Melanie Taylor wanted to go with her husband to see their son, Lance, but her drinking had increased again and Sherm told her there was no way she could visit Lance in Southern California that fall. He wouldn't take her because she'd only add to the problems he already knew he'd have upon his arrival.

Melanie was furious.

Madison told her dad she'd look after her mother, for pay, of course, and Sherm decided it would be worth the money. Getting Lance out of his current difficulty was important.

The phone call had come Friday night after Sherm had gotten home. Lance used the one call he was permitted to make from jail to call his parents.

"You're in *jail?*" Sherm had yelled when Lance called. "What did you do this time?" His blood felt like it was boiling.

"Marijuana isn't that bad, Dad. I shouldn't have been arrested. They shouldn't have put me in jail."

Sherm knew his blood had reached the point where it might explode from his veins and arteries and tried to calm himself down. After all he and Melanie had done to get the kid into college, making a donation to the school, pledging that Lance would do scholarly work, absorbing all the expenses Lance incurred, and they were increasingly numerous, Lance had screwed up, again. He'd been arrested for smoking and possessing marijuana.

And to top it off, Lance didn't seem to think he'd done anything wrong. Wrong? It was *illegal*. He could do serious jail time.

Maybe we should just let him cool his heals in jail a week or two, Sherm thought to himself. That might be the best way to teach Lance a good lesson, that he can't keep breaking laws. He said this to Melanie and was greeted by wailing and a flood of tears.

"You can't do that to your own son!" she screamed. "We've got to get him out of jail."

Sherm relented and made flight reservations for the next morning. At least I'm going to let him stay in jail overnight, he said to himself.

After Sherm rented a car, he drove to the county jail to see Lance, found him looking disheveled and almost shaggy, and was glad Melanie hadn't come. "So what happened?" he asked his son.

"Not much. A bunch of us guys just had a party. Nothing special. But I guess one of the neighbors complained about the noise and the police showed up. We weren't being loud but the old lady wanted to get us into trouble." Lance tried to lean back in the visiting room chair but the chair didn't budge. "When can you get me out of here?"

"I'll have to get a lawyer for you first. I called our attorney last night and he's finding one for me."

"So when can you get me out of here?"

Sherm could taste the bile in his throat. "As soon as I can. Your 'nothing special' party may take a little time to clean up. I realize patience is an unfamiliar quality to you, but I think it's about time you learned about it." He pushed back his chair to leave, then called the jailer.

Lance stared at his dad in disbelief. "You mean I have to stay here in this crappy place?"

"Kind of looks like it."

The jailer took Lance back to his cell as Sherm watched. Tiredness suddenly overwhelmed him as he walked to the visiting room door. He hadn't slept well the night before and his flight had left at 6:25 a.m. from Sea-Tac Airport. Having driven from the John Wayne Airport directly to the jail, he still needed to find a hotel and remembered one he'd seen on his way. It had looked decent enough, he thought, and made his way back to it. Relieved to find lodging, he went to his room, called his Seattle attorney, and got the name of a local lawyer he recommended. "Of course, it's Saturday so I doubt he'll run around for you today. Maybe tomorrow."

Sherm thanked him and left a message for the recommended lawyer. Then Sherm lay on the bed and was asleep in three minutes.

Late afternoon Sherm was awakened when his phone rang. The attorney, Roger Blaine, told him he'd come to the jail Sunday afternoon to see Lance but it would be Monday before he'd be able to get him released. "I'll need to post bail, Mr. Taylor. You okay with that?"

Sherm assured him he was. "And call me Sherm."

After they set a time to meet with Lance, Sherm called Melanie. Madison answered the phone and then handed it to her mother who said, "How's Lance? Did you get him outa jail?" her voice was slurred but Sherm had no trouble understanding her.

"He's doing fine, dear. Looks good and was treated well in jail. It didn't take long to get him released. I'd hand the phone to him, but he's taking a shower. I knew you'd want to hear right away so I called. How's everything going with you?"

"Fine, jus' fine. Madison takes good care of me. When

are you an' Lance comin' home?"

Sherm paused before answering, trying to figure out how to explain not getting on the next plane. "I think I need to go to Lance's school while I'm here, just to be sure Lance is doing well, which I'm sure he is. Of course, I can't call them until Monday, and that's okay because Lance and I can spend some time together." He wondered how his lies were coming across to his wife. She expected Sherm to bring Lance home, and that certainly wasn't going to happen, at least for awhile. "I'm not sure he'll be able to come home immediately because of his classes, Melanie."

Melanie didn't say anything so Sherm continued, "I'll let the office know I'll be gone." Melanie still didn't say anything. "I'll keep in touch." He paused again, "And please try not to drink too much, Melanie." He heard a click as she hung up.

That didn't go too well, he said to himself as he hung up his phone. But it would have been a whole lot worse if he'd been honest with his wife and told her the true situation with their son. Probably he shouldn't have said anything about her drinking, though.

Sleep had made him feel much better, but now he realized how hungry he was. He hadn't had anything since a cup of coffee and a donut on his way to the airport hours before.

After showering and changing, he headed to the lobby and asked the attendant to recommend a restaurant. Without hesitation, the young man suggested The Hamilton Restaurant and Lounge. "It's just a couple blocks east of here so you can walk if you don't want to drive. They have wonderful prime rib and there's an adjoining bar if you enjoy a drink before dinner."

Sherm thanked him and decided to walk, as the attendant had suggested.

As he left the hotel, Sherm felt as though his feet were shuffling and he had trouble picking them up and putting them down. His large flat feet, often slow, always a bit clumsy, had plagued him as a kid, making playing sports a problem during the years he wanted to play football and baseball. Tonight his head felt as slow and weary as his feet. And his heart was just a heavy lump pulsing blood from the top of his six-foot frame to the toes of his long feet.

How did this mess happen? What had gone wrong with the beautiful blonde boy they had raised? Everything had started out with such promise. Lance had been so smart, garnering praise from his primary teachers, one of their favorite students he and Melanie were told. And then came junior high and a slow decline in grades, a rapid escalation in truancy, and a gathering of friends neither of his parents liked or appreciated. The angry tirades of Melanie and Sherm were matched by the silent rebellion of their son.

And now he had landed in jail. What would happen next?

His thoughts switched to Melanie, dear, beautiful Melanie. How he had loved her as they watched their children grow and his business develop. What had happened that she drank so much he couldn't bring her with him? What had he done, or what hadn't he done? He'd asked himself that question a million times before tonight as he'd watched her addiction mushroom. Somehow he'd failed her.

And Madison? He couldn't be sure she was taking care of her mother. She may have been trying to get money or steal something to sell, a skill she'd grown adept at. Somehow he'd failed her, too.

He reached the entrance to the restaurant and headed to the lounge.

THE SCOTCH went down smoothly and Sherm ordered another. The lounge had only a couple of stools at the bar, one of which was next to him, and when someone sat down at the empty seat, he didn't look up until she said, "Hello."

Hello, such a simple word, but her voice had the loveliest sound, low and yet melodic as though, when saying hello, she was singing the word. Sherm realized the Scotch, quickly downed on an empty stomach, had affected him more than usual and that her voice really wasn't melodic and she wasn't singing, but he wanted to talk to someone, and someone had said hello. He returned her greeting as he looked at her.

"Hello," he replied. "Can I buy you a drink?"

Sherm was surprised she hesitated. He thought she'd immediately accept.

"Thanks, but I don't think so. Frankly, I just wanted a chair to sit on and decided to get a Perrier while I waited for a table." She laughed. "I was told it would be awhile since it's Saturday evening." The bartender brought her water. The lady commented, "I don't think he's happy with me. I'm supposed to order something more expensive I guess."

Sherm looked a little closer at her as he replied, "Yes, probably so, perhaps a Manhattan? Or martini? Who comes into a bar and orders water?" he asked as he laughed. "My name's Sherm, by the way."

"Rebecca Stewart. I'm a pharmaceutical representative in town for a company meeting and it's been a long day. I'd hoped to have a good meal and not have to wait, but that's the way the day's gone." She sipped her water. "What about you?" she asked. "Here for business?"

"No, unfortunately. I came down to see my son, Lance. He's having some problems." He ordered another Scotch just as Rebecca was called to her table.

"Why not join me?" she invited as she slipped off the stool. "I don't like to eat alone in a restaurant, and I think you'd be good company." She laughed again.

"I'd like that," he told her, and Rebecca told the restaurant host there would be two at her table. "I'm not sure I'll be good company, though. You saw the glasses lined up at the bar," he said.

Following Rebecca into the dining room, Sherm noted she was a few years younger than he and a few pounds heavier than Melanie, but she had what he always called "a nice walk," a term he used as he watched the women in his office. He liked her light brown hair reaching past her shoulders.

He ordered a prime rib steak and she chose the same. "I'm fed up with salads," she commented as she loaded her baked potato with butter, sour cream, chives and bacon bits. "After what I went through today, I deserve more substantial food."

Sherm thought about Melanie and the light fare she always ate, constantly worrying about weight gain. Sherm enjoyed watching Rebecca satisfying her healthy appetite.

As they ate and drank, they talked about the worlds they lived in. Rebecca told him she was based in the Portland area and had the Northwest states, including Alaska, as her territory. That meant she travelled a lot.

"I'm okay now about always getting on a plane and going somewhere, but one day I'm sure I'll get so tired of it that I'll find something else to do. The money's too good right now, though." She'd ordered a glass of Pinot Noir and took a sip. "Every month I load up my 401k and add to my personal savings. When I retire, I intend to do whatever I want." Sherm heard the laugh he enjoyed so much.

Sherm told her about the trouble Lance was in and his wife in Seattle, but he didn't mention Melanie's personal problems. He told her about his work and how well the lending business was going. "Why don't you buy a house?" he asked.

"And have to take care of it and mow the lawn and weed the flowers in my spare time? I don't think so. I like my apartment and the freedom it gives me. If the neighborhood gets run down, I can move and I don't have to wait for a sale. If a repair is needed, I call the manager. Like I said, I like the freedom." Then she paused before continuing, "I owned a house once, that is, my husband and I did. In our divorce he got it. I didn't want it."

They visited long after they'd finished their prime rib dinner and dessert. After finishing her wine, Rebecca declared she was worn out and needed to get to bed before catching her plane the next morning. "My car's in the parking garage," she said as they walked to the restaurant lobby.

"Will you have breakfast before your flight tomorrow? Perhaps we could meet here again." Sherm tried to be nonchalant as he made the suggestion.

Rebecca didn't accept his invitation right away, and Sherm began to think she wouldn't. Then she said, "Well, perhaps coffee. I'm not sure I'll be hungry. But I've enjoyed our visit very much and it would be nice to see you again. Say 9:00? That would give me time to drive to the airport and check the rental car back in."

As Sherm walked back to his hotel, his feet seemed lighter and his step quicker.

CHAPTER 26

At 9:00 the next morning Sherm had been waiting for 15 minutes at a table at The Hamilton Restaurant when Rebecca arrived, casually dressed for her flight home. She spotted him immediately, drinking his coffee and looking at a menu. "Just coffee," she told the waiter as she walked to Sherm's table.

Sherm got up to greet her. "Did you sleep well?" he asked in a pleasant tone.

"Yes, I slept very well. Was it the wine, the food, or the great conversation?" She smiled at Sherm as they both sat down, and very quickly the waiter brought her coffee.

"What will you have? I think I'll have the Sunrise Special and my coffee." Sherm had on a sport jacket with his shirt opened at the neck.

"Just coffee. I can't eat a bite," Rebecca replied.

They talked further about Lance, and Sherm reminded her he had a one o'clock appointment to meet the lawyer at the jail. "I'm surprised he's meeting us on a Sunday afternoon. But I'm glad about it. I'll need to put up bond money to get Lance out of jail, hopefully tomorrow. This is all new to me. I guess I'm lucky to have some resources to help my son, including a Seattle lawyer who provided the name of the lawyer here. I would have been flying blind."

The hour went by quickly.

Just as Rebecca was leaving, Sherm asked if she'd give him her telephone number. She looked at him, lowered her eyes, and then scribbled a number on her business card before handing it to Sherm.

"I'll call and let you know how everything works out," he said. Rebecca didn't answer.

BEFORE SHERM met the attorney, he called Melanie but got no answer. He left a message telling her things were going well with Lance and him.

Then he called Annie to tell her he wouldn't be in town for a few days. "I'm sure you can handle any problem that might come up, Annie."

"Are you all right?" she asked. "Has something happened?"

"Things are fine. I'm just taking a few days off. I'll call Brian and tell him to postpone any appointments from the last seminar." Following Annie's call, he phoned Brian.

He didn't have Angela's home number and told himself to be sure to remember to call her Monday.

I guess I've done everything I can, he thought to himself. Now if Roger Blaine can just get Lance out of jail.

By the time he drove to the jail, it was one o'clock and Roger arrived at the same time as Sherm.

The two men talked before seeing Lance, and Roger explained the probable scenario on Monday when Lance might appear before a judge. "Has Lance been arrested before on a drug charge?" he asked.

Sherm shook his head. "Not to my knowledge."

"Then I think he might not have to do jail time. What he did is illegal. Smoking marijuana is a Federal offense, but in California the level of offense is low, especially if it's the first time. A lot depends on Lance's behavior before the judge."

"That might be a problem. He doesn't seem to realize he's in trouble."

"Hmmm. Well, let's go talk with him."

Lance's demeanor hadn't improved overnight. "I thought you'd get me out of here by now," he complained when he saw his dad. "Is this the lawyer you got me?" he asked as he looked the man over.

"I'm Roger Blaine, and your father has retained me to represent you," the attorney volunteered. "I'm going to ask you some questions, Lance. There are a few things I need to know before I decide how to proceed. Okay?"

Jail didn't seem to be working to improve Lance's personality. He grunted at Roger.

Roger ignored the obvious character flaw. "Have you ever before been arrested for a drug violation?"

"No."

"Tell me about the party and your arrest."

Lance repeated much of what he'd told Sherm about the incident, again citing his opinion that he wasn't doing anything wrong and that "the old lady just wanted to make trouble."

Roger asked a few more questions and then rose to leave.

"Are you going to get me out of here now?" Lance questioned.

"On Sunday? Kind of hard. I'll get things started tomorrow morning."

Lance furiously started to attack Roger as Sherm pulled him back. "You get me outa here!" Lance yelled at the lawyer. The jail attendant rushed over, grabbed Lance and headed back toward his cell, Lance all the while still yelling at Roger and Sherm.

The two men found a bench and sat down. Sherm put his head down, with his hands cupping his forehead and his elbows on his knees. "I don't understand my son.

He's had a bad attitude, but not this bad. I'm sorry," he apologized.

"Do you realize Lance is probably suffering from withdrawal?" Roger asked solemnly.

"What? You mean he's addicted?" Sherm stared in disbelief at Roger's words.

"I think so. And I also suspect he's probably been using something stronger than marijuana." Roger waited for Sherm to adjust to this news and then continued. "This is what I want to do. I want to keep him here at least overnight and then see how he is tomorrow. I can arrange for bail tomorrow, but I'm not sure that's the best thing to do. I don't want him to go before a judge before he's ready to 'adjust' his behavior." Sherm noticed Roger emphasized the word. "One insolent word will completely destroy our defense. Are you okay with that?"

"I'm okay with it." Sherm shook his head. "What do we do after he's out of jail? I suppose his continuing here in school will be out of the question."

"Probably. He needs to get treatment, Sherm. He'll only get worse if he doesn't."

The two men sat in silence until Roger stood to leave. "I'll call tomorrow morning and we'll meet again. Okay?"

Sherm nodded and as Roger started to walk away he said, "Thank you, Roger."

Sherm continued to sit alone on the jail bench for a few minutes before he stood and slowly walked to the entrance door and headed to his car. When he got back to the motel, he called Rebecca.

ON MONDAY when Sherm and Lance's attorney met at the jail they briefly conferred before seeing Lance. "A lot depends on your son this morning and how he behaves," Roger told Sherm. "I can't help someone who thinks he knows more than the authorities. He's got to be at least a *little* sorry for his behavior."

The additional time in jail seemed to have improved Lance's attitude. Sherm and Roger were pleased he had decided to cooperate. Sherm posted bail for him and Lance was released into Sherm's custody.

At the hotel Lance showered, shaved and changed into a suit, shirt and tie they'd purchased enroute. "It's so good to be clean again," he commented as he preened in front of the mirror. "I never want to go to jail again."

"I guess you know that'll be up to you," Sherm replied as he finished getting ready for dinner.

Lance continued quietly admiring his appearance.

Sherm decided it was a good time to talk to his son while the jail experience was fresh. He'd probably never have this good an opportunity again, and he went straight to the point. "You've got to get clean inside, Lance, and stay clean. I hope you see this as a wake-up call, and I hope this one experience will be the only one you need because I'm not going to come running again to bail you out of trouble." He looked at Lance for a reply, knowing it was important for Lance to think and then respond to his words before he said anything more.

Lance quit looking at himself and silently looked at Sherm for several minutes. "I don't know if I *can* quit, Dad," he finally replied. He sat in a chair and lowered his head. "I'm not at all sure." His words were muffled, but Sherm understood. "I want to quit drugs, but it's so hard. I don't want to ruin my life."

Sherm listened and wondered if Lance was trying to con him. He was direct again. "Are you trying to fool me into believing you're really going to try to make something of your life?" he asked.

"No," replied Lance with a choke in his voice.

That was all Sherm needed to hear. From that moment on he resolved to be the father he'd wanted to be before all the wrangling and fighting got in the way. He and Lance had the most intense and productive conversation they'd had since Lance's junior high days.

Afterwards, Lance said, "I need your support, Dad."

Sherm answered, "You have it, son."

Roger proved to be a skillful attorney and Lance received no jail time for his violation. Sherm and Lance had talked about Lance's school and, before they flew home, they both went to the college to withdraw Lance from all his classes.

Sherm was momentarily surprised to learn that his son was failing every single one of his studies, but then he realized it was an "of course" kind of surprise. How could Lance abuse drugs and do well in his classes?

CHAPTER 27

When Annie got Sherm's call on Sunday afternoon, she was surprised. He and Melanie usually set their vacation times well in advance so he could finish all the appointments and loan closings around those days. This time Sherm seemed to have forgotten he was heading into a busy week.

She talked with Brian Duke, and he was equally surprised. "I'll be on the phone all day trying to re-schedule everything," he complained. "And we don't know when he'll be back in the office. What a dufus," he commented and then said, "Annie, I didn't mean that. Sherm's a great guy, but I just don't understand his pulling something like this when it's such a busy week."

She checked with Angela at ten o'clock and found he hadn't called her. "You'll need to call escrow if he's got loan closings in the next few days to make sure everything's fine. I'm sure you'd do that anyway."

Angela seemed upset. "Of course I would," she snapped.

Annie shrugged her shoulders after the call. She couldn't care less what Angela would do or would not do, but then she thought about the borrowers. They didn't need to be hurt. She cared about them.

At lunchtime she went to the cafeteria and sat with other loan processors to eat. Still upset with them, she'd decided that ostracizing herself wouldn't get her information she might want. And she was desperate to find out anything that would help her and Stephanie.

The conversation was mostly about television shows she wasn't interested in, and she quickly ate her Top Ramen noodles and walked back to her desk. As she sat down, she looked up and saw Monica Sullivan, the "spy," as Annie thought of her, approaching her cubicle.

She sat down in the chair next to Annie's desk. "I see Sherm's gone today. Will he be back soon?" she asked without greeting Annie.

How rude, Annie thought. "I don't know," she answered and gave no explanation.

Monica seemed irritated with Annie's response and frowned. "You don't know if he'll be in today?"

"He won't be in today. I don't know when he will be in." If Monica was going to be rude in her approach, then Annie could be rude in her response.

Monica didn't seem to notice Annie's lack of friendliness. "Well, when he does come in, would you please tell him I need to see him?" She smiled and said, "Thank you."

Why did she need to see Sherm? The mystery of Monica's presence deepened. What was she trying to find out? Was she intending to ask Sherm about Annie? It all sounded like a circular firing squad to her and she was the target in the middle.

It had been almost a week since her visit with Stephanie. Time for a phone call she decided and reached for Stephanie's phone number at the school.

Stephanie sounded frustrated when she answered and said, "I've been over at Jose's house again, but I can't get any more information. He just repeats what he's already said, and that isn't going to help us at all."

"I guess he's told us everything he knows." Annie didn't want Stephanie to know how discouraged she herself was, so she volunteered her findings about the fraud going on at Franklin. After looking around to be sure no one was watching, she lowered her voice and said, "I've found all sorts of evidence showing loan documents are being changed. It's so blatant I can hardly believe it. Justin was right. But I can't see any reason for anyone here to have killed him. As I told you before, killing someone for their accounting work doesn't make sense."

"You're right," Stephanie apologized. "But I'm so sorry you're in the middle of all the fraud going on, Annie. You're a good person and I know you wouldn't be part of it. Justin was right about you."

They hung up after visiting a little more. The conversation had improved Annie's disposition that day, just because Stephanie believed she was an honest person.

But Annie felt so much anger inside herself. Anger at everyone at Franklin Mortgage. The other processors, the loan officers, Monica Sullivan, Sherm Taylor, Angela Albright, and especially Carter Brislawn. She thought about Carter and the meeting she'd had with him. He should have gotten on top of the fraud evidence, not ignore it. She was more furious with him than anyone else because he had the responsibility to investigate what Annie had told him about. Instead, he'd as much as accused her of being jealous. She almost shook when she thought about him.

Maybe he'll be killed by a drive-by shooter, she thought. Then she scolded herself. What is happening to me that I want someone else to get hurt?

When she went home that afternoon, Annie hugged each one of her children as she greeted them. "I love all of you so much," she told them.

Hardly any part of her work had made her happy that day. Everyone had disappointed her. But the most important people in her life, her family, hugged her back and said, "We love you, too, Mom."

CHAPTER 28

Carter knew all about the changed documents, and he'd known for sometime. It didn't bother him at all. As all the other employees committing fraud were doing, he rationalized the fraud by telling himself he and other employees were making dreams come true, were providing means for people to own their own homes, were important players in a dynamic process. What if people couldn't get loans to purchase houses? The whole economy would go into a kind of relapse.

Of course, he had no intention of pursuing Annie's claims about Angela who was doing what Sherm told her to do.

Monica's presence had started to irk him as he noticed her conversations with processors, loan officers and accounting personnel. What could she be discussing with them? Was she finding anything he didn't want her to find? Surely not, but it was a possibility as she visited so many people.

CARTER'S JOB as CEO of Franklin Mortgage meant that he commit considerable time visiting other offices that were part of the company. At first he found it exhilarating to be introduced to everyone and to have the power that went with his position. However, it didn't take long for the visits to dull, his presentations to branch management to be uninspiring, and his patience with the questioning listeners to dwindle. His accounting acumen overcame any other leadership skills he might have developed, and all that truly interested him was the bottom line of the branch offices. Were all the people performing? Were goals being met? Was more money being made each month?

Carter didn't concern himself with being liked. And he didn't concern himself with how underwriting guidelines were followed.

If a branch office wasn't making money, as far as Carter was concerned the employees might as well have been building boats. He had no interest in the branch and its improvement, and, in fact, recommended to JWColbert management that the office be closed.

The employees were of no consequence to him.

Carter was the antithesis to Al Pendleton. Al Pendleton would have made sure all his people were trained and helped. He would have done everything possible to avoid closing an office.

The branch manager of an office the CEO recommended closing often repeated his conversation with Carter. "I asked Carter what kind of severance package he would suggest for the employees, and Carter answered, 'None.' I laughed and asked him again. His reply was, 'Evidently you didn't hear me when I said none.' I realized then that he was serious. And I knew I was going to be out on my ear unless JWColbert came through."

The one thing Carter enjoyed about going to various cities in the Pacific Northwest was being able to search for real estate values. It there was good value in a property, he often bought it.

His high-rise condo in Seattle had never been listed for sale, but he had buyers wanting to make offers at prices in years past he would have thought obscene. Now he thought the value was greater than the offers because the condo had wonderful views of the city and harbor. He liked living there.

CHAPTER 29

When Monica Sullivan came to Seattle and Franklin Mortgage, she'd had a confidential mandate from her supervisor at JWColbert: Find out if Franklin Mortgage is engaging in fraudulent mortgage loan practices.

Subprime loans in particular had been mentioned when he talked with her.

Monica's background in fraud detection was perfect for this assignment, and she had expected to need all the knowledge she'd gained in her many years' experience to detect any dishonesty in the mortgage originating company. She'd need to look at the accounting records, but uppermost in her search would be the necessary combing of loan documents to make sure they complied with lending standards.

Her cover story was very simple and quite plausible: She had been sent to streamline operations in any way possible following the purchase by JWColbert. At the time, Monica had laughed at her alleged purpose because JWColbert itself needed streamlining in its communications within every department of the investment company.

By late fall of 2007 Monica realized she didn't need all the experience she'd acquired. She merely had to watch the loan officers and processors. She could *see* them committing fraud.

What she didn't know was how pervasive the fraud was. Were all of the loan officers involved? Were all of the processors guilty? Her search shifted from whether there was fraud and how it was done, to who was doing it.

And that was a problem. Identifying the perpetrators was taking time.

Monica's conversation with Annie hadn't been helpful, and Monica easily could tell that the loan processor hadn't intended to be helpful. So far, Monica hadn't found Annie to be dishonest, and she was inclined to feel Annie was a good processor who wasn't involved in all the cheating going on at the company. She had no idea why Annie was so angry.

The person Monica wanted to find out about was Sherm Taylor. She had no proof of Sherm's involvement, but she'd found plentiful evidence against Angela. Obviously, Sherm was a productive loan officer, and perhaps Angela was under so much pressure to get his loans approved that she made changes in the numbers and in signatures. But Monica doubted she'd done so on her own.

When Sherm returned from his Southern California trip, one of the first people to call him on the intercom system was Monica.

"This is Monica Sullivan, Mr. Taylor. I've been working on streamlining functions at Franklin, and I'm hoping I can meet and visit with you today. What time would be best?" she asked.

Sherm seemed surprised at her call. "Well," he said slowly, "I've been gone a few days and work has stacked up. Can we schedule our meeting sometime next week, say Thursday?" Before she could answer, he continued, "I'm not sure I'll be at all helpful with your mission. Probably Annie would be better."

"Oh, I'll want to visit with her also, but I'd like to get your impressions first. Next Thursday will be fine. Say 10:30?" She was the first to hang up the phone.

When Monica lightly tapped on Sherm's door and he responded for her to come in, she was in no mood to be bullied by the most productive loan officer at Franklin. Her personnel interviews earlier in the week had produced alarming results from lying individuals who had no problem telling her Al Pendleton had left the company in a mess and without any dependable lines of communication. She didn't believe these tales for a minute.

Monica dispensed with small talk this morning and came right to the point. "Mr. Taylor, I've been asked by JWColbert to explore ways to improve communication within Franklin Mortgage. You've been here a long time, I believe," she said as she looked at her notes. "When did you become a loan officer at Franklin?"

"Don't you have it on your paper?"

Monica frowned and said, "Mr. Taylor, we can make this easy or we can make this hard. Which would you prefer?"

Sherm stared at her before answering, "About eleven years ago."

"Thank you, Mr. Taylor. I think we're already starting to communicate better." She paused, smiled at him, and then said, "In those eleven years have you noticed ways we can make improvements in lines of communication within the mortgage company? Has it gotten more difficult since Franklin was purchased by JWColbert?"

Sherm answered her questions briefly at first, but as she encouraged him to respond in greater detail and then praised his observations, he relaxed and went on at length about his suggestions, even picking up paper and sketching several ideas he had.

Finally, she inquired about Al Pendleton's management style. "Was communication better?" she asked.

Sherm seemed to hesitate. He shifted in his chair. "I'm not sure how to answer that question," he said. "I think his style was unique because he and his wife started the company and had a close watch on it as it grew. Al seemed to know everything that was going on in the business— not just at Franklin Mortgage but in the entire industry. He talked to the employees here in Seattle and in all the other offices so he knew, in most cases, what people wanted and needed. Was communication better? you ask. It was different, I'd say. It worked during Al's ownership because Al was directly involved. It probably needs revamping with the new owners and management."

Monica noticed immediately that Sherm hadn't mentioned Carter Brislawn by name. But she agreed with Sherm's analysis of the difference in style and thought Sherm had presented it quite diplomatically.

"Thank you, Mr. Taylor. I very much appreciate your candor and help," Monica said as she rose to leave.

"We got off to kind of a rocky start I think. I should have suggested you call me Sherm." Sherm got up and opened the door for her. "Please let me know if I can be of further help."

As Monica walked to her cubicle, she thought how appealing Sherm was. She had no doubt that he was involved in the dishonest practices at Franklin, but she liked him.

Chapter 30

After Monica left his office, Sherm pondered her visit as he sat at his desk covered with files. What was her real purpose? Was she on a fact-finding mission about communication, or had she been sent by JWColbert to find out if Carter was doing a good job for them. Something about her questioning bothered him, but he couldn't put his finger on it.

Whatever had been the reason for her visit made no difference he finally decided. He had to get his work done.

The files continued to stay closed, though. Finally, he thumbed through several and hastily put them into two piles, one for Annie and the other for Angela.

His marketing specialist, Brian, had done a good job delaying the applicants who had attended his seminars. He needed to call them himself, though. Usually he enjoyed this part of his work, but today he kept postponing making the contacts.

He picked up the phone and reached a number on his speed dial.

"Hello," Rebecca answered.

"Hi," Sherm said. "I was thinking of you and decided to call. How're things going?" He shoved the files in front of him off to the side of his desk.

"Pretty good. I made a great contact today that I think will bring a lot of business my way," Rebecca said. "How are things in Seattle?"

"Good. Way too busy, though. I'm still trying to catch up from being gone." He played with the pen on his desk. "It's been hard to focus since I returned."

Rebecca didn't ask why. Instead, she said, "How's Lance doing? Is he getting treatment yet?"

"He seems to be doing okay. I haven't seen any evidence of his doing drugs. We're working on getting him into treatment at one of the places here." He hesitated and then said, "I'd like to come down to Portland this weekend. Will you be home on Saturday if I drive down early to see you?" He nervously waited for her response. Was he being too direct about wanting to see her?

In his mind's eye he imagined her holding the phone and contemplating what she should say, wondering if she should tell him to come.

He'd made the first advance. Would she accept?

"Yes, I'll be home, Sherm." She gave him directions to her apartment and they said goodbye.

He hung up the phone, then opened one of the files on the desk and dialed the phone number given. He was back in business.

CHAPTER 31

When Monica Sullivan, the fraud investigator, left Sherm's office late Thursday morning, Annie saw they were both smiling. I didn't expect that, she thought to herself. I expected them to be angry with each other. Sherm doesn't like being questioned, and Monica is a pretty aggressive woman it seems to me.

She was again surprised when Monica called her that afternoon and asked if Annie could go to lunch on Friday. "My treat," she said.

Annie said, "Sure." It would be a change from Top Ramen.

They met at a nearby restaurant Monica had suggested. "I think it would be best if we didn't leave together from the office. You know how it is," Monica had said.

Annie didn't know, but it was fine with her.

After the waitress had brought coffee and they'd ordered, Monica led the conversation away from the initial pleasantries. "You do very good work, Annie. I appreciate your thoroughness."

Annie frowned. So Monica was checking on her ability as a loan processor. Annie wasn't pleased.

"Thank you. But why are you looking at my work? Is JWColbert planning to fire some of us? Is that what you're doing here?" Annie asked with a sharp tone.

Monica smiled. "No, my comment was merely an observation, a compliment." She stabbed her salad with her fork. "I have the feeling that for some reason I've offended you, and if I have, I'm sorry. It was unintentional."

She looked at Annie and continued. "Sometimes I come across as being very aggressive, and I suppose I'm often abrupt. It's one of the things I keep reminding myself I need to be careful about. I'm not a man so I sometimes have to display a softness that's hard for me." Then Monica surprised Annie by laughing.

Suddenly Annie understood. Monica had been assigned to do a job usually done by a male. Managers would expect corporate to send a man to interview decision makers in a company. And men being interviewed wouldn't respond unless she showed strength and aggressiveness. In spite of all the progress women had made in the corporate world, financial services, including mortgage lending, was still a male-dominated world. Only a handful of departments at Franklin Mortgage were led by women, and no branch manager was female.

"I'm so sorry," Annie replied, flustered by the assumption she'd made about Monica. "I did think you were rude when you came by my desk. But I understand now. Can we start over?"

Monica laughed again. "That's the second time in two days I've started over after a rocky start. I've found I had to change tactics."

"Sherm?" Annie asked, knowing the answer before Monica nodded her head.

"He told me I should talk with you because you'd know more about communication problems. That's been my cover story, you know."

"Cover story?" Was this woman crazy?

"I had to make up a plausible story about my being sent here from New York. Communications are usually a problem when companies get bigger, and then when they're bought by a larger company, the problems grow. It seemed like a logical reason." Monica took several bites of her salad while Annie tried to grasp what she was hearing. "JWColbert really did send me here, but it was to find out if any fraud was occurring. That's my background, fraud investigation." Monica put her fork down and continued, "I'm telling you this because I've found flagrant fraudulent actions at Franklin Mortgage, but I don't believe you're at all involved. I think you're a good processor, like I said, and that you're meeting underwriting guidelines on your loans."

"But I really don't understand. Why are you telling *me*?" Then Annie interrupted herself, "You went through my files?"

"Of course. You leave them out on your desk and never lock your desk drawers."

"But you went through my files?"

Monica shook her head in exasperation. "Annie, you're the limit. I compliment you, and all you can say is 'You went through my files?' Of course, I went through your files—-I'm a *fraud* investigator!"

Annie finally took a bite of her salad, and then another bite. "And you're telling me this because?" she let the question hang in the air.

"Because I'll be getting a report in to JWColbert, and I don't want you to be worrying about what I write. Someone's going to figure out what I'm actually working on, I'm afraid, and if you hear about it, you might wonder."

"I see." Annie was finally enjoying her lunch.

"Have you been aware of all the white-out changes?" Monica asked.

"Yes. And I've been very angry about them. I'm still angry." Then she told Monica about going through Angela's garbage. Annie hadn't expected Monica to laugh so hard.

SHORTLY AFTER meeting with Annie, Monica scheduled an appointment with Carter. During all her investigation and interviews leading up to their meeting, she'd tried to determine whether or not Carter was part of the fraud. Was he being deceived or was he a part of the deception? Her instincts told her he knew a great deal about what was happening at Franklin, but it was possible he was so focused on the bottom line of the lending business that he failed to see what was going on around him.

When Monica entered Carter's office, he seemed intent on finishing paperwork in front of him before starting the interview and merely waved at her to take the chair opposite his desk.

Monica sensed this was going to be another power duel like she'd had with Sherm. She groaned to herself. She'd expected a steel door in front of her, and apparently that's what she was going to get.

After Carter put the papers aside, he looked up and said, "Well, I hope your investigation has produced some good ideas for streamlining our communication systems here at Franklin. I've always thought we had a very efficiently run operation, but I'm open for new suggestions. What do you have?" He smiled pleasantly but his eyes were masked.

"First, I want to thank you, Mr. Brislawn, for the courtesies your personnel have extended me during my stay. They've made themselves available when I've asked." Monica had earlier decided to make this her initial statement and smiled briefly as she acknowledged their helpfulness.

"I also want to say that you have very knowledgeable employees and several had extremely good ideas that

I'll be sure to incorporate into my report." Monica had no intention of saying anything further about what his personnel might have suggested. Let him guess, she thought to herself.

She shifted the conversation away from the report. "I got into the home loan business following a stint as a trainee at a New York bank. I enjoyed the idea of helping people own their homes and found the entire process very interesting. The secondary market is something most people don't understand, I feel." She wanted to change her position in the chair but refrained. She didn't want to convey any sense of uneasiness.

"How did you get into the lending business, Mr. Brislawn?" she asked. She tried to make her voice sound interested but not overly curious.

Carter looked at her without expression. For a moment Monica thought he wasn't going to answer, but then he said, "I'm not really sure. I've always enjoyed working with numbers and I suppose someone told me I'd do well in this field, Ms. Sullivan."

It flashed through Monica's mind it wouldn't have been likely someone would tell him he would do well working with *people*. That would have required a personality more interesting than a very clean, smooth rock.

In her Google search on Carter's background, Monica had learned about his father and grandfather and their boat building enterprise and carefully steered away from this topic. Instead, she commented on his alma mater. "Many of our New York employees are Yale graduates, and I understand you are also. Do you get back to visit?"

"Occasionally. It's not a long drive to Connecticut from New York when I'm in town."

Many people would have asked about Monica's college as a responding question, but Carter had nothing more to say or to ask.

She stood to leave and then, almost as an afterthought, asked, "Have you seen any evidence of people altering loan documents?" As she turned toward the door, she watched Carter out of the corner of her eye. "It's a temptation when an employee very much wants a borrower to qualify, so we're always on the look-out for dishonest behavior."

Anger fleetingly crossed Carter's eyes before he caught himself. "No, I haven't. Franklin Mortgage is operating very honestly." He stood but didn't walk Monica to the door as Sherm had. "I'll look forward to your report, Ms. Sullivan."

MONICA SMILED to herself as she left Carter's office. The interview had gone as she'd believed it would. His responses had been non-committal and devoid of expression until she'd hit a nerve regarding altered documents. Yes, she thought, he's up to his eyeballs in fraud.

Her report was in the mail to her supervisor the next day, and she was on a plane back to New York at the same time.

CHAPTER 32

As he watched Monica close his office door, Carter angrily banged the desk with his fist. She wasn't here trying to work out communication problems. He didn't believe that story for a minute. But was her last question the real reason for her visit? And what had she found?

For several minutes he sat at his desk, pondering possible answers. In addition, he wondered why corporate would have sent a woman for any fraud investigation. He didn't believe a female would be up to the task of discovery. She was smooth, though, he decided. She might have stumbled onto files that had been altered and was trying to find out if he knew about them.

Of course he knew. But in the culture of acceptance displayed at the JWColbert New York office he hadn't worried about what his subordinates were doing. As long as bottom-line figures kept going up, everything was fine.

What concerned him right now were home values in his personal portfolio, many coming in lower than he'd expected. He was finding it harder to sell at prices he wanted, and he was working hard to unload some of them.

He checked his accounts in the Caymans and was satisfied.

He spent no more time thinking about Monica Sullivan. She was gone and he was glad.

He picked up the phone and dialed the number he often called. "Hi, Eva," he said when the service answered. "Is Goldie available tonight?"

It was silent at the other end of the phone, and then Eva replied, "No, Mr. Brandt. Goldie is no longer available." There was a pause. "You roughed her up pretty badly the last time she came to your penthouse. I'm not sure we can serve you again."

Carter frowned. He picked up his pen and doodled on a small pad before saying, "I was upset that evening. It won't happen again, I promise."

Eva asked Carter to repeat his promise and then said she'd send someone to his penthouse apartment at 9:00 p.m.

Carter smiled as he hung up the telephone, proud he hadn't said he was sorry, happy he got his way without apologizing. He didn't care who came to his apartment. Once again he realized how powerful money is.

CHAPTER 33

Monica's report lay on her supervisor's desk. She waited for Alan Marks, head of the internal investigations unit of JWColbert, to comment on her lengthy review since he had sent her on her mission.

"Unbelievable," was his first reaction as he completed his reading. "Fraud being committed right in front of your eyes." He looked at Monica and shook his head as he started through the report once again. "And you believe Carter Brislawn knows all about it?"

"Yes, I think so. He's an unusual duck, not at all like his predecessor, Al Pendleton. In fact, I had a difficult time getting anyone to say much of anything about him, whereas they spoke very highly of Mr. Pendleton. Their omission said a lot."

She continued, "Most of the loan officers and processors are involved in the document changes, and the corruption extends beyond those offices. It's astonishing."

"Well, I'll get it to the higher ups and see what they want to do," Alan said as he closed the report file. "Good job, Monica."

ALAN MARKS got Monica's report to the next echelon at JWColbert, where it was received with displeasure.

"I warned you about that red-headed dame when you let Marks send her to Seattle. And now she's come back with a bunch of lies and claims about the personnel there. Carter's doing a great job and she has the nerve to fault his lack of personal contact with his people. *What?* They're doing a *job*, a good job. They're closing more loans than ever, and we're getting them packaged and re-sold in record time."

"Yes, you're right, and I'm sick and tired of her rants and witch hunts," came the reply. "She's all about loan prevention, I think. If it were up to her, we wouldn't be able to sell to our investors and the whole market would collapse.

"Stuff the report in a back file and forget about it. No reason for it ever to see the light of day."

CHAPTER 34

In the spring of 2008, several times since their initial conversation about fraud at Franklin Mortgage, Annie and her father had discussed it. Andy initially had a hard time believing it was occurring so blatantly, but Annie's proof was hard to ignore.

When Linda, Annie's mother, told her daughter she was concerned about Andy and how upset he seemed to be about something, Annie explained what she'd told her father. "I talked to him because I didn't know what to do, but I didn't want to worry you also, Mom."

"Did he tell you what to do, dear?" Linda asked.

"No. Anything I might do would bring all kinds of problems to the company, everyone who works there, and me." She waited a minute and then said, "I guess I'm just a chicken. I need this job." Annie felt like crying but it wouldn't do for her to burst into tears in front of her mother. After all, she was trying to protect her from worry.

"Well," said Linda, "the good news is that he's learning how the Internet works. He's talked and talked about it but never gotten around to actually searching for something."

"And you've worked with search engines for years, Mom!" Annie laughed. "Did you teach him?"

"Good Heavens, no! I tried, but it's something you have to learn by doing, I think."

The next time Annie talked to her dad in the computer room, she asked him what he'd been searching for on the Internet. "And did you find what you wanted?" She had a huge smile on her face when she asked.

"Your mother been talking to you?"

"She's worried, Dad. Because you seem worried. I told her about the fraud at work."

"Oh. Well, I didn't want to tell her until you said it was okay. And, yes, I found a whole lot out when I did some searching. The lending business has changed so much, and not for the better," he seemed very sad. "Someday soon the whole thing's going to come down, and no one's going to know who owns what mortgage. It's gotten to be like a food chain when a loan is made. The prospective home buyers go to a mortgage lender and get a loan. Then an investment bank buys that loan and lots more from mortgage lenders. The investment bank packages the loans together and sells to investors who take parts of the package. In the meantime, the home buyers send their payments to someone else who gets an income stream from payments. How will it all get sorted out when everything comes crashing down? When all the bad loans come due?" Andy paused for breath. "I can't imagine," he finished and shook his head. "It's going to be like a Rubic's cube. Awfully hard to solve."

Annie took her father's arm as she saw the expression on his face. "Dad, you have to let it go. You can't dwell on what you think might happen. Everything's going to be okay. There are regulations…."

Andy continued to shake his head. "The laws have changed, Annie. Regulations have changed. I loved banking when there was some rhyme and reason in the industry. But now I'm worried about what's going to happen, and I'm worried about you working at Franklin. I want you to quit. Get another job." Andy looked at his daughter with concerned eyes.

"I called my friend Al," Andy continued.

"Al Pendleton?"

"Yeah. We've talked a couple of times the past month, and he's as worried as I am. In the year since he sold Franklin, things have gotten worse, and to add to the problem the credit market has exploded and banks are using a lot greater leverage. Neither of us see a good ending to it all." Andy became quiet and then again told Annie, "I want you to get another job."

"I can't, Dad. I need this job. Where else would I get the income I do now? If things are as bad as you think, every mortgage company would have the same problems, wouldn't they? And loan processing is what I know. It's what I *do*." Annie's head suddenly hurt and she pressed her fingers against her forehead. She wanted to take an aspirin.

"Your mother and I will lend you money until you can find another way to make a living."

"What? Are you serious?" Annie felt her head was splitting.

"Yes, I'm very serious. And very nervous." Andy looked closely at his daughter and his eyes were sad. "You know I'm right."

Annie didn't comment further as she and her dad walked back into the living room. The twins were playing with Legos her parents always brought out for them, Gage and Taffy were watching a movie on TV, Rachel was on her cell phone, and Linda and Brad were in the yard looking at the forsythia and tulips. Everything seemed the same, but it was all different. Fraud at Franklin and an ominous future had darkened Annie's day, and she couldn't shutter the fear away.

CHAPTER 35

Annie recognized John and Sally Cramer the minute she saw them in the mortgage company lobby. They were the borrowers she hadn't been able to qualify for a loan but Angela had. Annie had discovered Angela's duplicity when she'd seen the Cramers at the escrow office.

When her telephone rang, for some reason Annie wasn't surprised to hear that the Cramers wanted to see her. The receptionist was apologetic. "I know you don't usually see borrowers like this, but they're very insistent."

Annie walked out to the lobby and greeted the couple. She saw a small empty office, the same one she'd greeted Stephanie Diamond in, and motioned for the Cramers to follow her. "It's nice to see you, Mr. and Mrs. Cramer. I hope everything is going well for you." The now familiar headache was returning.

"It's good to see you, too, and please call us John and Sally," the young woman said. "But we're having big problems with our mortgage loan, and we're hoping you can help us." Sally was almost apologetic in her tone.

"What's wrong?" Annie knew the answer before she asked.

"We've gotten behind in our payments. And last Friday I lost my job, so we'll probably get further behind. The payments are just too high." She looked at Annie as though she were accusing her.

"I didn't finish work on your loan, Sally," Annie objected, sensing she was going to get blamed for the tough spot they were in. "Angela did, you'll recall."

Sally backtracked. "Yes, I remember. Sherm told us you were so busy that he was assigning our loan to Angela. We never did understand why we couldn't have you doing the processing. We liked you much better." Sally seemed close to tears and her husband took her hand.

"Annie, we brought copies of papers we originally signed and copies of the final documents." John picked up where his wife had left off. He spread papers out in front of Annie.

Annie looked at the documents. She remembered the papers Sherm had handed her the day he'd assigned the file to her. But she hadn't seen the final documents the borrowers received. Of course, they didn't reflect changes Angela had made, only the loan amount, interest rate, payments to be made. The Cramers would have no idea what changes Angela had made. It all seemed so unfair. Because of Sherm's greed and Angela's duplicity, they were going to lose their home. Their dream was being killed.

Annie didn't know what to say.

"Have you talked with Sherm?" she asked after some hesitation.

"No." Sally answered. "We've tried and tried, but he's always out of the office, and he never returns our calls."

Annie sighed and then said, "He's been gone a lot." She didn't make an apology for him. Sherm should have called back.

"Who has your loan now?" she asked, knowing Franklin would have sold it to another company.

John read her the name on the latest paperwork they'd received.

Annie knew she had to be very careful about what she said. "I think you should try to call this number," she told them, pointing to the phone number listed on the paperwork, "and try to negotiate your payments downward. In the meantime, I'll talk to Sherm." Annie picked up the papers in front of her and handed them back to John. "I wish I could be more helpful. I'm sorry."

John and Sally thanked Annie but their eyes were downcast as they left, with John's arm around Sally's waist.

Annie raced back to her desk before the tears started to fall. She felt so helpless. Borrowers were starting to feel the effect of her co-workers' actions, and Annie could do nothing about it. Putting her hands against her aching forehead and her elbows on her desk, Annie let herself cry.

BEFORE ANNIE left for the weekend, she tried calling Sherm again but couldn't reach him and left a message. "Please call John and Sally Cramer. They were in the office today. Is there a way they can refinance at a lower rate?"

Brian, Sherm's marketing assistant, had called her before that to tell her he was having trouble contacting Sherm about the results of their most recent seminar. She noticed Angela's "to-do" pile was getting shorter, as was hers. What was Sherm doing with his time?

When Annie reached home, the first thing she did was to remind Gage to walk Taffy. "He's locked in all day, Gage. We're lucky he's so good about waiting to go outside."

"Can I walk him over to Tony's?" Gage asked.

"No, that's too far. Stay in our block." Since Gage had celebrated his 11th birthday, Annie had noticed early signs of teengeritis and the resulting quests for independence. She and Brad usually tried to work out a compromise acceptable to the three of them.

"The twins are staying with friends and will be gone until Sunday morning," Annie continued.

"Good. I don't know why anyone would invite the brats, but it's fine with me," Gage answered, happy with the news.

"Gage! You don't mean that."

"I don't? They're always bugging me."

"One day you'll realize you love them."

Gage shook his head. "I doubt that," he said.

Annie refrained from lecturing her son. She'd done that before to no avail.

Saturday, when Annie and Brad decided to look at houses for sale, Rachel had invited a girlfriend over for the weekend, and she was told to stay home with her brother. "Call if you have a problem. We'll have the cell phone."

Rachel didn't protest because she and her friend had already planned to listen to their iPod music.

Annie was relieved to have solved a problem so easily.

After spending several hours looking at houses for sale, Annie and Brad stopped at a Dairy Queen for soft cones. "It's easier without the kids, but it's still tiring," Annie complained as she licked the chocolate from the top of the swirl. "Did you see something you really liked?"

"It seemed like the prices have started to come down. I liked that," Brad answered as his tongue lopped an inch off the large cone. "You remember the next to the last house we saw? Well, it's down $5,000 from last month."

"I didn't realize that." Annie thought about the Cramers. Were they going to have to sell at a lower price than they'd bought? Had housing prices topped out?

As he enjoyed his ice cream, Brad continued talking about the houses they'd seen. "Are you hearing at work about prices coming down?"

"No, not really," Annie replied.

Brad looked at her as he said, "Sometimes it's hard to see the forest."

"What?"

"I mean that when you're in the middle of something, it's hard to see what's happening. Your viewpoint is skewed. Maybe you're too much inside the bubble to see that you're inside a bubble." Brad finished his cone.

"I'm too close to the housing and mortgage industries?" Annie countered.

"Exactly. You hear all the propaganda put out by people selling houses and mortgages. I don't. I can look at things differently."

Annie thought Brad sounded superior, and it made her angry. "Well, you don't know anything about it," she told him as she tossed her head. Her ice cream was melting faster than she could eat it, and she dabbed her chin with a napkin. "Anyway, I didn't see anything I wanted to buy."

Brad said, "I didn't either, so we'll just keep saving our money. Something will come on the market, and we'll be ready."

CHAPTER 36

Carter combed his curly brown hair and goatee before he left his private bathroom at Franklin, thinking about the latest production report he'd been scanning. The numbers were down, and one of the major contributors of the decline was Sherm Taylor. Carter frowned. Sherm had been a loan officer he could depend upon for growth.

When Carter called Sherm, he got Sherm's answering machine and curtly spoke his message. "When you get this, come to my office." He didn't think he needed to say anything further, and he expected Sherm to respond immediately.

It was the following morning when Sherm knocked on Carter's office door.

Carter's stern face showed his displeasure at having to wait for Sherm. "I expected you yesterday," he said briskly.

"I wasn't in the office so didn't get your message." Sherm's voice didn't sound apologetic.

"Don't you listen to your messages?"

"Not always."

"Well, you should." Carter plucked the production report from his desk and read Sherm's monthly figures. "Your production has been down for three months. Why?" Carter didn't wait for an answer before continuing, "And you've been out of the office a great deal. Obviously, you're not working outside the office, trying to get more business." Sherm's attitude wasn't making Carter more pleasant.

"Loans are harder to come by, Carter. And I've been

busy with personal matters," Sherm replied, shifting a little in his chair.

Carter stared at him. "What are you telling me? You're saying that when this market is clearly continuing to head upward, you're taking some time off? Is that what I'm hearing?"

"I'm not sure it's still heading up, Carter. I read a lot of the same things you read, but I'm not sure they're an accurate barometer of the market. I don't have the same good feeling you do."

Carter's voice was sarcastic. "You think you know more than JWColbert does. You think you know more than the three rating services. You think you know more than all of Wall Street." He now sounded disgusted as he said, "I don't think so."

"Time will tell who's right, Carter," Sherm replied in a voice that showed no hesitation. "But I'll try to spend more time on the business."

Carter was so furious that he almost sputtered. "That is what you're *supposed* to do. You're supposed to be working." He thrust the production report against his desk. "I'll expect better numbers this summer."

As Sherm left his office, Carter continued to fume to himself. He needed more production. He needed larger bonuses. The last phone call from his boss at JWColbert had pointed out the same numbers he'd been seeing.

Carter looked out the large window in his office and watched the ferry to Bainbridge Island. He'd been so busy with his properties that he hadn't been able to spend time at his island home. Nor had he visited his parents on Mercer Island although they'd called several times. Next weekend he'd go to Bainbridge. He didn't give a thought to seeing his mother and father.

CHAPTER 37

The last time Andy Carmichael and Al Pendleton had visited had been two months earlier when Al told Andy that he and Gretchen were planning a lengthy trip to Europe the summer of 2008. "It's been something we've both wanted to do, Andy. We won't leave until the middle of May, but summer is supposed to be nice 'on the continent,' as they say."

Andy had said it was a good idea for them to travel while they were both healthy.

News of the tour bus accident was slow to reach Andy, but when he learned of Gretchen and Al's deaths, he immediately called Annie.

"Boy, is it hard to believe. They work all their lives and then 'Boom!' they're gone so soon after retirement. Well, at least they had a little time to travel around the States and see some of the world," he told his daughter.

"You should do the same thing, Dad. Take that new car out beyond Seattle. I think a few trips would be good. Mom would enjoy getting out, too."

Andy sighed. "That's what your sister told us. Said we should drive to Montana to see her and her family. But you do know, don't you, it's your mother who doesn't want to drive there?"

"No, I didn't know."

Annie asked Linda about it. "You've got a brand new Buick and you never leave King County. Why not, Mom?"

"Because I'm worried your father will fall asleep while he's driving."

"Really? He's that bad?"

"He is," Linda confessed. "I keep poking him and asking, 'Are you awake, Andy?' And he answers, or it's more like a grunt, 'of course.' And he's angry with me for even asking. So I discourage him from driving to Montana or anywhere else, for that matter."

The conversation worried Annie. On top of the problems at work, the fraud she'd seen, the visit by the Cramers, and the death of Justin, she could hardly bear thinking her dad might be having health problems. Well, she wouldn't think about it. Nothing was going to happen to Andy, she told herself. But then she followed that thought with the news of Al and Gretchen Pendleton's deaths. She hadn't thought they'd die either.

She often thought about Justin Diamond. Every time she saw someone from accounting Justin's face appeared in front of her and she imagined what his last minutes might have been like. Who was he facing? What were his last words? Was he angry? Was he afraid?

The more she thought about Justin's neighbor, the more she felt he was the key to solving Justin's murder. How could Annie help Jose unlock the mystery of who was talking to Justin on that fateful morning? A huge brick wall seemed to block her progress.

She had kept in touch with Stephanie even though neither had anything new to report.

Summer meant the children were out of school, and Linda was coming each day to take care of them. Annie knew it was too much for her mother, but she didn't know what to do about the situation. Rachel wasn't dependable enough.

It was one more thing on Annie's mind each day, one more worry.

CHAPTER 38

Spring had blended into summer for Sherm as he tried to keep his marriage to Melanie afloat while spending as much time as he could in Portland with Rebecca. Melanie's drinking was worse than ever, but he couldn't convince her to get treatment at one of the good rehab centers in Seattle.

The bright spot in Sherm's Seattle life was Lance, as he slowly began conquering the drug problem caging his future. If he failed to accept his addiction and get help, Lance knew he'd slip further down the rabbit hole of daily doses and constant oblivion. Inch by inch he began his long recovery, knowing it would be a life-long journey.

Sherm began to see the little boy in his life return as a young man.

When Lance told his dad he wanted to enter college in the Seattle area, Sherm asked if he could help by contacting one of his clients who was on the college board. Lance turned him down. "No, Dad," he said. "This is *my* problem."

Sherm proudly accepted Lance's reply.

Madison, Sherm's daughter, had brought up low grades and planned to enter nurse's training after her senior year. Sherm felt he didn't know her as well as he wanted. They passed each other in the large house, but other than for friendly greetings they had few conversations.

Melanie had no idea about Lance's addiction because Sherm hadn't told her. She relied on Madison, who seemed to be compliant, to care for her during Sherm's frequent absences from home.

As Sherm drove to Portland, following the Renton "S" curves on 405, passing the exit to Sea-Tac Airport, travelling the busy highway heading south through the Nisqually Flats and across the Columbia River Bridge, his thoughts criss-crossed the people in his life and where his path had taken him the past months, a path that had led him closer to some and farther away from others.

He thought about Franklin Mortgage and his neglect of clients and their needs. He thought about Carter and the anger of the company president. He realized he felt bad about letting clients down, but he wasn't remorseful about Carter's problems. Carter was a jerk and should never have been in charge of the mortgage company. He had no idea why Al Pendleton had put up with him.

One of his biggest concerns was the housing market and the nagging belief it was going to come tumbling down. If it did, how would his personal loans be affected? He had been making good money and was getting debts paid, but was he still too much in debt? If people couldn't get home loans, he wouldn't continue to get big checks.

As he pulled into Rebecca's driveway and set the parking brake, he had one last thought before getting out of the car. What would happen to Melanie if he left her?

Once he entered Rebecca's home, though, all thoughts left his mind except his happiness to see the woman he loved. As she kissed him in response, he knew she felt the same way without her saying a word.

As THEY enjoyed cocktails and dinner, Rebecca and Sherm often talked about their work and the stresses they experienced, sharing more with each other than they'd been able to with anyone else.

"I feel so, well, liberated when I talk to you," Sherm told Rebecca. "It's like I can really express myself for the first time."

"I feel the same way, Sherm."

"I guess years ago I talked with Melanie and told her all about my work, but it's been so long I can hardly remember it," Sherm said as he sipped his wine and plunged his fork into the pork chops Rebecca had fixed. "We had Lance and Madison when Melanie and I were not more than kids ourselves, and pretty soon we just talked about them and what they were doing. Never much about what we were doing." He took a bite of pork and expressed his pleasure at the taste. "These are great chops. How did you fix them?"

"Like I always do, in a slow oven, soup and crumbs over the top."

"Well, they're delicious." He scooped out more mashed potatoes onto his plate and ladled gravy over the top before he continued. "Lance is doing so well now that I can hardly believe it. I wanted to help him get into college, but he told me, basically, that he had to handle things himself." He took another sip of wine. "I wish Melanie could appreciate how well he's doing, but she can't appreciate much of anything these days. Except her booze." Setting his glass down, he said, "I've given up on helping her." He looked at Rebecca. "I want to be with you."

Rebecca smiled. "And I want to be with you."

Expressing his doubts about the housing industry, Sherm continued the conversation. "I know so many people say we haven't reached the top of the cycle, but I don't agree. I have the feeling we already have but just don't know it. JWColbert is screaming for more mortgage loans and seems to have the funds to get them into the secondary market, but I've backed off and made sure I'm not over-leveraged personally."

"What do you think is going to happen?" Rebecca asked as she rose to get their dessert.

"Who knows? Franklin's president says to write more business. But Carter Brislawn's always said that, and he's never himself written a mortgage loan, never looked a borrower in the eye. He's always been part of management, telling us what to do and what not to do."

Rebecca had just pulled plates from the cupboard and stopped. She turned, looked at Sherm and asked, "Carter Brislawn is your boss?"

Sherm heard the incredulous tone in her voice and said, "Yeah, why? Do you know him?"

Putting the plates on the counter top, Rebecca walked back to her chair. "No, I don't," she said, "but I have a friend I met at the gym who was married to him."

"He was married? I didn't know that."

"Well, it's no wonder he doesn't tell anyone. He beat up my friend, more than once she said, and she had to get a restraining order. She got a divorce, too."

Sherm couldn't think of a word to say other than "Wow."

"It's been years since they were married, but she's still got some scars." Rebecca said softly. "I thought his name was very distinct so remembered it. My friend said his father and grandfather had the same name."

"That's what I've always heard. They're in the boat building business. Well, I guess his grandfather, Carter Brislawn I, is dead, but Carter Brislawn II is alive and well on Mercer Island." Sherm shook his head. "I always thought Carter was an odd person and kind of a jerk, but I didn't know he beat up women." He was silent a moment and then exclaimed, "And to think he's head of a mortgage company! Al Pendleton should have done a little more due diligence on him."

"Who's Al Pendleton?"

"The man who started Franklin Mortgage. Hired Carter some years ago, and then when he sold the business to JWColbert, he put in some good words for Carter and Colbert kept him on as company president." Sherm felt himself getting angry. "JWColbert should have done better due diligence, too. But all they wanted was a cash cow to milk, and they've been good at that."

Rebecca laughed. "Milking a cash cow? That's a vivid description."

"Accurate, too. Until now. It won't go on forever, and I think it's coming to an end."

"I asked what you thought was going to happen, and now I want to know what you'll do." Rebecca got up again to get their dessert. "Will you keep on writing loans or find something else to do?"

This was a question Sherm had started to ask himself.

"I don't know, sweetheart. I've worked in this business for so long I don't know what else I can do. I'll just wait and see, I guess." Sherm thought about all the changes he'd made and had asked Angela to make on loan documents during the last months, and it was dawning on him that one day his fraud might be discovered. No, he told himself, that wasn't going to happen. No one was going to go back over his loans.

He was a good salesman and knew he could find a job.

"Are they hiring in pharmaceuticals?" he asked Rebecca as he smiled.

ON THE return drive to Seattle, Sherm's mind was on two people: Rebecca and Carter. He couldn't figure out how he was going to resolve his dilemma over taking care of Melanie and loving Rebecca. He knew he had to reach a solution, and reach it soon. He remembered hearing years before that not being able to resolve conflict might eventually lead to insanity. He felt himself getting closer.

Thoughts of Carter Brislawn were another matter. No dilemma or conflict of emotions there. Carter's violence had been a new disclosure, but Sherm had no doubt about its validity.

As he drove north, he thought about how he and Annie used to talk and share ideas and news. He missed those times. Well, he decided, he was going to try to mend fences, regardless of how Annie saw his methods of writing loans. He'd have a frank talk with her, maybe take her to lunch.

Even to himself, Sherm couldn't admit he had been committing fraud. He'd just been trying to help clients get mortgage loans to reach their dreams of home ownership. What was wrong with that?

His muddled mind shaped his contorted view of what he'd been doing the past months, personally and professionally. How much the need for money had played into his decisions was not something he focused on. Supporting his family and himself was just part of life and he accepted that. What he had forgotten as a salesman was the possibility of getting his foot caught in the door. Rebecca's door.

CHAPTER 39

When Sherm called Annie into his office on Monday morning, she thought perhaps he meant to fire her. His business was down, and obviously Angela was doing the kind of loan processing he preferred, the magic kind, so Annie would be the employee to let go.

Sherm was smiling at her when he said, "I'm wondering if you have lunch plans, Annie, and, if you don't, I want to take you out. We used to visit over lunch in the past, and I'd like to do that again. Can you go today?"

This wasn't what Annie had expected. She was flustered when she answered, "Well, yes, I can go." Then she decided to be direct. "Are you going to fire me?"

Sherm's smile broke into a guffaw. "What? You think I want to take you to lunch so I can fire you? No, no. You've got it all wrong. I just want to talk."

A relieved Annie said, "Today would be a good day to go. The lunch I packed won't be any better a week from now than it is today. The kids got the last of the peanut butter and the fresh bread, so it was going to be Top Ramen again."

Sherm laughed even louder.

Annie felt happy hearing his laughter. Being able to visit with him over lunch would be a good thing. She had missed their chats.

They chose a nearby restaurant and agreed to walk there since it was a warm day.

As they later left together, Annie saw Angela out of the corner of her eye. She imagined a black cloud over

Angela's head. *Stop it!* she told herself. But it was hard to quit smiling.

Sherm ordered a glass of wine and suggested Annie order one also, which she did. After searching through the menu, Sherm told the waitress he'd like the braised beef over noodles. Annie ordered a hamburger and fries and saw Sherm grin.

"Are a hamburger and fries okay?" she asked.

"Of course. They just reminded me of someone else who would have ordered the same thing," Sherm responded as he thought of Rebecca.

Sherm asked Annie about her children and Brad, and Annie then asked Sherm about his family. Their answers were of the non-disclosure kind, nothing too personal.

After they were served their wine, Sherm raised his glass in a toast. "To good friends," he said, and they both sipped. The coating in her throat felt good to Annie. She relaxed.

"We used to have lunch together every couple of months, Sherm. Before everything got so chaotic." Annie took another sip of wine. "I've missed those times." She thought about the changed documents and wondered if Sherm intended to bring up the subject. She decided she wouldn't say a word about them even though her opinion of Sherm had changed. She liked him, and she probably always would, but fraud made a difference in her trust.

"I have also, Annie. And I think the last few months have been hard on our relationship." He took a gulp of wine, put the glass down a little harder than needed, and the liquid splashed up the sides. He seemed to hesitate slightly before saying, "You know what's been happening on my loan documents, don't you." He made it a statement and not a question.

Annie didn't know what to say so merely nodded 'yes.'

"You're too good a processor not to know. But I've got to tell you that I'm really sorry I let things get so out of hand."

Annie wanted to say that it was more than letting things get out of hand. It was fraud. She started to respond, but the waitress brought their food.

"Can I get you anything more?" she asked.

Sherm requested another glass of wine for both of them.

"Oh, I don't know, Sherm," Annie told him. "I'm already feeling the effects of the glass I have."

Sherm nodded to the waitress. "We'll each have another glass," he repeated. He turned to Annie and said, "There's nothing on your desk more important than this conversation is, Annie, and, if you have to take a taxi home, I'll pay. I want to talk." He lifted his almost-empty glass and drained it.

Annie just silently looked at Sherm.

"We've been going through a rough patch the past few months, and I feel bad about it." He paused and then said, "I know you don't approve of what I've been doing to some of the loan documents." Sherm had an unhappy, bitter look on his face.

Annie almost felt sorry for Sherm. Almost. Not quite. She determined not to say anything but to let him grovel a little longer. He deserved whatever regret he was feeling. He deserved having a hard time admitting what he'd done.

"Right?" he asked.

Annie nodded her head.

"You'll have to admit I've gotten people loans for houses when no one else would have been able to," Sherm said.

Annie raised her left eyebrow but continued to say nothing.

"Oh I know you think you're better than me because you wouldn't have done the same thing!" Sherm sounded desperate.

Annie broke her silence. "Not true, Sherm. I'm not better than you in any way. But what you've done is fraud, plain and simple. And I didn't want any part of that."

The waitress brought their food and two glasses of wine. Sherm lifted his glass and took a husky gulp. "I didn't think of it as fraud when I was doing it. I was just trying to help people with their dreams," Sherm replied, using the age-old excuse.

Annie shook her head as she said, "That's what everyone's going to say when all these bad loans blow up. 'Just helping people with their dreams.' It will be a chorus." She cut her hamburger into two pieces and took a bite of a French fry.

"I think the market's going to come apart, Annie. And it's going to happen fast. We've already seen Countrywide get scooped up, and I hear Bank of America is starting to cry the blues because they mistakenly thought they'd gotten such a good deal when they bought the company." Sherm continued to focus more on his wine than on his food. "I'm worried."

Annie was surprised at Sherm's candor. "Do you think all the bad loans will be uncovered?" she asked. "Are you worried about that?"

Sherm hesitated. "I don't think that will happen unless the crash is very, very bad."

"'The crash?' You're calling it a crash?" Annie was surprised. "You sound as alarmed as my dad. Do you honestly think it will come to that?" The wine was starting to affect her thinking, and Annie put the glass down in favor of picking up her hamburger to take another large bite.

"No one knows, and those who're supposed to know aren't talking. It's all a guess, but I'm guessing it might be pretty bad. As you're aware, I'm not doing many loans. And those I'm doing have to be very strong."

Annie didn't know if it was the wine or if it was Sherm's conversation, but she was starting to re-think her previous opinion. Maybe Sherm had figured out what he'd done was very wrong and wanted to make amends. Should she tell him about Monica Sullivan's accusations? She decided not to make him worry about that also.

She hadn't liked the way she'd felt about him. She wanted things to be the way they had been. For some reason the song *The Way We Were* popped into her head. She smiled at Sherm as she said, "You're really feeling bad, aren't you?"

"I feel like a louse, not only about my loans but my personal life. I'm not going to get into that, but I had to talk to you about the business and try to set things straight again for us. Are we okay now?" he said in an almost pleading tone.

"Of course." Annie was puzzled by the look on Sherm's face and the questioning tone of his voice. She decided there was a lot more going on in Sherm's life than she knew about, but she also knew it was probably none of her business.

Obviously relieved, Sherm changed the subject. "Say, I heard Carter was married years ago. Did you know that?" He started working on his food instead of drinking his wine.

Annie was glad to see Sherm eat his lunch but was surprised at this news. "Nope. Who would ever want to be married to him?" she asked in a disgusted voice. "I can't imagine."

Sherm laughed. "Well, someone did and paid a big price for her mistake. He beat her up, left scars, and she had to get a restraining order against him even after they were divorced." He attacked his food with relish.

Annie thought about this information for a minute. She'd known Carter was unpleasant and couldn't care less about how loans were generated, but violence? This was a different side of Carter, a new dimension to his life. *The secret life of Carter Brislawn III.*

"We all have secrets, Annie," she heard Sherm say.

"Yeah," was all Annie replied to his comment. How many more secrets did Carter have? "I wish Al hadn't sold the company," she remarked almost as an afterthought. "If he hadn't, he'd probably still be alive to lead us through this mess."

"This mess had started before he sold, Annie. I wonder if he hadn't seen it coming."

"We'll never know." In a way, Annie was glad Al wasn't there to see what she and Sherm feared was coming for Franklin Mortgage. As they finished their lunch and left the restaurant, Annie was also glad she and Sherm had had "the talk," as Sherm would have called it. Sherm had eaten enough crow for her, even though it still upset her that he'd changed loan papers.

CHAPTER 40

It was early September, 2008. School had started and the three younger Robinson children were home on a weekend.

"Quit bugging me!" Gage yelled at Cammie as she stuck her tongue out at him. "Mom, let me beat her up!" he begged his mother. "She won't leave me alone."

Annie listened to Gage's request that he'd made probably one million times before and said "no" once again. Then she told Cammie to get the Old Maid cards out and she'd play with her. Cammie raced to her bedroom to get the game, then laid them before her mother.

"You have to shuffle, Mom," Cammie said.

"You need to learn how, Cammie. Just try it a few times," Annie told her as she handed the deck back to her daughter. "And did you see how Candy is doing when you went into the room?" Annie questioned.

"She's asleep. The bucket's next to her bed," Cammie said. "It's got puke in it." Cammie parted the deck and then tried to reassemble the cards into one pile. They spilled onto the table and she tried again. They fell chaotically. "See, I can't do it, Mom," she said disgustedly.

"Well, I'll deal this time and then I want you to try it again." Annie dealt each of them a hand and said, "As soon as we finish, I'll check on your sister. It's good she's sleeping. I don't want you to get the bug she's got so you'll sleep with Rachel tonight."

"Rachel's going to scream when I tell her that." Cammie said happily. She tried to shuffle one more time and then announced, "This game is dumb. Let's play Candyland. Okay?" When Annie nodded her head, Cammie raced upstairs to her room and ran back down again with her favorite game.

From in front of the television set where Gage had his Xbox connected, he said to Annie, "See how she gets away with everything? She gets her way every time she wants something."

"Do not," Cammie replied.

"Do, too."

"Do not."

"Kids, kids, don't start that," Annie objected. "Cammie, I'll play one game of Candyland with you and then it will be time for lunch. Toasted cheese sandwiches."

"Yummy!" both kids said.

After the game and when the sandwiches were ready, Annie said, "Cammie, call your dad to come and eat," Then she added when Cammie opened her mouth to yell, "No, go in the den and tell him."

Cammie got as far as the door to the den before yelling to her dad that lunch was ready.

"Where's Rachel?" Brad asked as he gobbled down his sandwich.

"At her friend's house, studying she told me."

"Yeah, right," Gage said. "Her boyfriend's over there, too, I bet."

"Yeah," Cammie agreed. "I heard her talking to him."

Annie put her sandwich down just as she was about to take a bite. "You're sure?" she asked.

Both kids nodded their heads.

"Well, I'll have a talk with her when she gets home." Annie said and then looked at Brad. "Or perhaps you'd like to?"

"Sure. It's about time she got the idea that we don't lie to each other around here, especially to parents," Brad answered. "She's been pushing the envelope for awhile."

"What's pushing the envelope mean, Dad?" Cammie asked.

"It means she's been getting as close to disobeying as she can get," Brad said.

"You've been there *forever!*" Gage told his sister.

Cammie stuck her tongue out at him.

Brad laughed, but Annie shook her head at both children.

The conversation gave Annie an idea, though. Sometimes we assume things and the assumptions are wrong, she thought. We think people understand what we say, and they don't.

"Brad, will you be home with the kids this afternoon? I want to visit Stephanie Diamond if she's not busy. Candy just needs to stay in bed and sleep. Gage and Cammie can play or watch a movie." She looked at both kids, "And you *will* behave."

Annie had the tone in her voice that always commanded obedience. Gage and Cammie nodded their heads.

After calling Stephanie, Annie drove to her home.

Stephanie greeted her enthusiastically. "It's been awhile since I've seen you, Annie. How have you been?"

"Fine, just fine. And you?" Annie asked.

"Doing okay."

Annie got right to the point of her visit. "I've been thinking about your neighbor, Jose, the one who saw Justin's killer that morning. Have you talked with him recently?" she asked.

"We nod at each other when we're outside, but I haven't been over there for awhile." Stephanie had a puzzled look on her face. "Why?"

"We never actually asked him if he could identify Justin's killer if he saw him again." Annie accepted the cup of coffee Stephanie handed her. "Sometimes I have to be very direct with my kids or they don't get the significance of something or don't know why it might mean something to me. And with Jose there's a language barrier. Do you think he might not have known to volunteer that he would recognize the man, and we didn't think to ask him?"

"I don't know," Stephanie replied. "We need to ask him," she said as she reached for the telephone.

Tony answered the phone and invited the two women to their house. "Dad's here now," he said.

Before Stephanie and Annie could decline her hospitality, Maria had brought them coffee and pastries. Although they weren't hungry, the pastries were appetizing and both accepted.

"Jose, we have a question for you about the morning you saw someone talking to Justin," Annie began, aware that Jose was looking at her expectantly. "We didn't ask you before, but we're wondering if you could identify him, either in person or from a picture. Do you think you'd recognize him?"

Tony translated so Jose would be sure he understood correctly, and then Jose nodded his head and said, "Si senora." Tony also nodded his head and repeated "Yes."

Smiling broadly, Stephanie and Annie looked at each other and then at their three friends. "Thank you, Jose!" they exclaimed at the same time.

"This is wonderful news, Tony," Annie said.

"Do you have someone you want my father to look at?" Tony asked.

Annie and Stephanie shook their heads and Annie said, "No, not yet. But I think we will. Just knowing Jose can make an identification really helps a lot."

Jose said something to Tony in Spanish who then translated, "Would it help to know what kind of car the man drove?"

"It would be wonderful! Do you know, Jose?" Annie said.

"Si," Jose replied. "El Porsche, blanco."

"A white Porsche?" Stephanie repeated.

Annie sat stunned. She knew only one person with a white Porsche, and he had known Justin Diamond.

They finished their coffee and pastries before leaving, thanked their friends, and returned to Stephanie's home.

Crossing the driveway between the two houses, Annie imagined Justin talking with his killer. In her mind she saw Carter Brislawn III with a gun.

At Stephanie's door she asked a question, "Do you know of any accounting work Justin was doing at home for people?"

Chapter 41

In response to Annie's question, Stephanie had said Justin did a little work for people but she didn't know what it was and who it was for. "He didn't talk about it much. We were both busy with our jobs and, when we weren't working, we tried to talk about other things."

On her way home Annie thought about Stephanie's answer and decided Justin must have purposely kept a lot of what he was doing from his wife.

"I don't think Stephanie had any idea what Justin was doing," she told Brad and then added, as she looked at Brad out of the corner of her eye, "Sometimes we don't know the person we're living with and what they might be up to." Sternly she questioned him. "Are you doing anything you're not telling me about? Something I wouldn't like? Are you hiding money from me?" Then she laughed and her dark curls bounced as she said, "Actually, with our kids around, neither of us would be able to get away with a thing, sweetheart. And they'd certainly tell us when we were getting close to the edge of the envelope." She paused and thought and finally said, "I think our kids are our secret weapons to honest lives."

At work on Monday, Annie sorted through brochures about Franklin Mortgage following its purchase by JWColbert and the subsequent hiring of Carter as company president. She remembered a picture of Carter shown in a publicity shot after his selection and plucked it from the folder in her desk drawer. This is a good likeness, she decided, and Jose can tell if Carter is the killer.

Carter was out of town again and Annie was glad she didn't have to see him in the office. She still needed to have Jose verify the picture.

She thought about how smug Carter had been when she'd told him about the fraud in his company. She was almost gleefully anticipating his response to a murder charge. She and Stephanie would contact the police and Jose would identify Carter as the man he'd seen that early morning. The police would arrest Carter and his evil world would come tumbling down.

What? she said to herself. What am I thinking? I must be getting neurotic. The police won't be involved because Stephanie won't let them be. And I promised Stephanie I wouldn't involve the police. So even if Jose identifies Carter, will he get away with killing Justin?

Once more Annie felt herself frustrated by events beyond her control. It had been a long road to finding Justin's murderer. She wasn't going to let Carter Brislawn III escape justice. She didn't know what Justin had done, but she now thought she knew what Carter had done.

CHAPTER 42

Annie brought the picture to Stephanie who recognized Carter immediately. "Carter Brislawn." Stephanie said.

"Yes. I think he's the man who shot Justin," Annie stated. "I believe he and Justin were involved in some kind of money-making scheme. I don't know why Carter decided to shoot Justin, but I've recently discovered he's a very violent man. Not at all the great person people think he is."

"But just because he's violent doesn't mean he shot Justin," Stephanie argued.

"No, but I'm convinced he did. If Jose can identify him, we'll know for sure." Annie could tell that Stephanie wasn't convinced. "And he drives a white Porsche," she added.

The look on Stephanie's face changed. "Let's go," she said.

When Stephanie and Annie took the picture to Jose, he became very excited as he nodded his head quickly and said, "Si, este es el que." Again, Tony translated, but both women had understood Jose's identification of Carter as the man Jose had seen the morning Justin was killed. There seemed to be no doubt in Jose's mind.

Tony asked, "Would you like my father to come to the police station? It would be very hard for him, but he would do it for you."

Stephanie started crying, but she shook her head. "No, Tony. Life is hard enough for your parents. I don't want them to be in trouble because he was willing to help me. I wouldn't feel right about it. Thank you, though, and please thank your father and mother." She dabbed a handkerchief at the tears in her eyes.

Annie added, "Since we now know who shot Justin, we'll find a way to bring the killer to justice. You've been very, very helpful. We wouldn't have had a clue who murdered Stephanie's husband without your help."

After they'd returned to her house, Stephanie broke down and wept. Annie tried to comfort her and then decided to let her cry it out, to let go of the months of wondering who had shot her husband at that early hour and how he had died. Stephanie needed to release her emotions.

"Would you like me to leave?" Annie finally asked.

"No, no, Annie. I'd like you to stay and talk to me unless it upsets you to see me behaving like this."

"Of course not, Stephanie."

They sat silently for a few minutes before Stephanie said, "I haven't wanted to believe Justin was involved in something illegal, but everything points to it. He and Carter must have been working together. I don't have any idea what they might have been doing."

"I'm sure you've been over every conversation you had with Justin prior to his death, and he never gave any indication of some money-making scheme."

Stephanie shook her head. "There was never anything."

"Well," Annie began as she searched her own mind, "what would they have needed each other for? Carter is such a loner, never with anyone at work unless they're in his office, really an independent guy I always thought. Unless someone had a skill he needed, I doubt he'd partner with them." She scratched her head and then continued. "Justin was an accountant, and a very good one I always heard. Would Justin's accounting skill have been necessary to Carter?" She looked at Stephanie as she asked the question.

"I don't know. Justin did his master's work in international accounting of some kind. I never really understood it. He wanted to work on Wall Street, but that didn't work out so he took the job Al Pendleton offered him. He still wanted a Wall Street job in international finance, though. I know a few times he set up overseas banking accounts for people when they asked him to." She got up and looked out the living room window.

Annie felt so sorry for Stephanie. Their conversation didn't flow as it usually did, and Annie hesitated to press her more quickly. She thought the answer to Justin's involvement had to be his accounting skills, though, and maybe it was the overseas banking that was the clue. She sat quietly, puzzled at Carter's need for anyone's accounting skills when Annie had felt this was Carter's expertise, looking at the bottom line of all reports.

"Do you have Justin's files? I mean the ones where he set up overseas banking accounts for people?" she asked Stephanie in a quiet voice.

"Yes, they're in a file cabinet in the den he used for an office at home. I haven't needed to look in it since he died, but I think I saw the key in the desk drawer. Should we check right now?"

"I'd like to, but I need to call Brad to make sure everything's okay at home. I showed him Carter's picture and told him what we planned to do, and he'll want to know if Jose identified him. I'll call while you check on the key. Okay?" Annie excitedly said to Stephanie.

Brad told Annie all was going fine at home. "What did Jose say about the picture?" he asked.

"He's our guy. Jose had no hesitation identifying him."

"So are you going to the police?"

"I'll tell you about it when I get home," Annie replied, not wanting to talk further while at Stephanie's.

Stephanie had a key in her hand when Annie walked into the den and was working on a lock to a black metal file in the corner of the room. This room must have been used only by Justin, she thought, judging by the light brown walls, the accounting and business books on the shelves, and the fishing pictures displayed. She noted a collection of Civil War volumes and asked Stephanie if that period of history was particularly interesting to Justin.

"Yes, he loved studying the Civil War, and, in fact, we took a trip one year to visit as many of the battle fields as we could. I didn't think I'd ever get him to leave the Gettysburg area." The key in her hand didn't work on the lock so she tried another one. "I've thought I should find someone with an interest in the Civil War period who might like his books."

The key turned in the lock and Stephanie pulled out each of the drawers. "I didn't realize he had so much material in these files. He must have kept every single piece of paper he ever brought into the house." She noted the file dividers, "And he was so organized. He has several client files, and they're all subdivided with the work he's done for them. I'll read a couple, 'Samuel Rogers, Accounting Statements, Taxes; McKinley Company, Accounting Statements, Taxes.'"

She looked at Annie and said, "I had no idea he did so much work outside Franklin Mortgage." She sat in the desk chair. "Here, take a look for yourself." Her voice sounded tired.

Annie rifled through some of the files, looking particularly for one labeled Carter Brislawn III. She found none and felt devastated.

"I don't see anything having to do with Carter. Either he didn't keep records or there weren't any records to keep. That's hard for me to believe, though." Annie lowered her head.

"Maybe Justin wasn't working with Carter," Stephanie's voice held a glimmer of hope. "Maybe Carter was just angry about something and he didn't mean to shoot Justin."

Annie jerked her head up to look at Stephanie but couldn't bring herself to tell her friend what she was thinking: Sure, Carter just happened to have a gun in his hand when he went to your house early in the morning and he just happened to shoot Justin for no reason at all.

Instead, Annie said, "Well, I think we've had a full day, and I'm sure you're very tired. This has to be very difficult for you." She reached over to take Stephanie's hand. "Try to get some rest and we'll talk later."

Annie couldn't wait to talk to Brad about the day's events.

WHEN ANNIE got home and told Brad the whole story about Justin's murder, his probable dishonesty, and then her promise to Stephanie that she wouldn't involve the police, Brad was furious.

"*What!* You've actually found the murderer and you can't go to the police to prove Justin wasn't killed by a drive-by shooter? What are you and Stephanie thinking? Of course, you should tell the police so they can arrest Carter! Jose has said he'd identify Carter and that's been the major problem. You need to talk Stephanie into doing what's right." His jaw was set as he talked, and he moved his arms for emphasis as though Annie wouldn't get his point otherwise.

"Brad, Brad!" Annie yelled. "It won't do any good for you to wave your arms around. I'm not the one you need to convince. It's Stephanie." She lowered her voice when she saw Candy and Cammie looking at her. "I made a promise to her and I intend to keep it. There's got to be another way to work this problem out and get Carter arrested."

Annie thought about the file cabinet and all of Justin's records with the exception of anything having to do with Carter. There just has to be something, some kind of evidence Justin kept, she thought to herself, and then said to Brad, "Justin did a lot of corporate and tax work for people he knew, but when we looked in his home office file cabinet, we couldn't find anything having to do with Carter. Where do you think he might have kept Carter's files, honey?" Then she added, "You men think alike."

Brad smiled at his wife. "Really? *Really?* Carter is rich. Obviously, I don't think like him or we'd be living in a big house we own on Lake Washington. And have lots more houses we rent. Isn't that what you've told me about him?" He came over and hugged his wife. "I can't even afford one house for you."

Annie hadn't intended to hurt her husband with her comment, but he'd taken it to mean she thought he should do a better job providing for her.

"Oh, honey, I didn't mean you should think like Carter does about his money. I'm happy the way you think, I mean I'm happy the way you are. I don't want you to be like Carter," she said, exasperation in her voice. "I just want you to help me find where some files might be." Then she added, "And I'm talking about where *Justin* might have put files. Somewhere Stephanie would find them but no one else would."

"Umm," Brad replied. "Well, let me think *like a man*," he said, and he grinned again. "I'd put them in the garage maybe. Underneath paint cans. If I died, you'd probably never find them, though. You don't like to paint."

Annie laughed at him. "You're right. They'd be there when I moved." She watched Brad scratch his head. "Where else do you think Justin might have hidden them?"

"Did he have a hobby? Some guys would keep 'their secrets' where they spend time working on something they like. Books of butterflies? Stamps? Coins? Coins, that's a good one because they could make money their wives wouldn't be aware of. Trading cards?"

He saw the excited look on Annie's face and stopped.

"Books," she said. "He's got a collection of Civil War books and memorabilia in his office. He might have put a file among them that no one but Stephanie would be likely to find." She looked at Brad and laughingly said, "See, I told you you'd figure it out, and you did."

"I hope so, but you'll need to call Stephanie and ask her to look under paint cans in the garage and in a bunch of books in his office before you know for sure." He looked at the twins. "Life with your mother is exciting, girls."

"Yeah, sure, Dad," they chorused in voices that sounded like they totally disagreed with their father.

"Do you have a coin collection, Dad?" Cammie asked. "Is it under paint cans in the garage?"

"Or butterfly books?" Candy chimed in.

Annie looked at her husband and shook her head. "I'm going to call Stephanie and you can take the girls out to the garage and show them your stamps and other interesting things under the paint cans."

CHAPTER 43

When Annie talked with Stephanie, she explained how she and Brad had come to the conclusion that Justin probably hid records in a place Stephanie would discover but no one else would.

"I'll look right now in the garage and in his Civil War stuff and call you back," Stephanie told an excited Annie.

It took Stephanie no more than ten minutes to telephone Annie and tell her she'd found records in the Civil War book collection. Eagerly she said, "It's all here, Annie. The corporate files, tax returns, everything. Justin did an enormous amount of work for Carter and he kept records of all he did."

"I want to come over, but it won't be for about an hour. Will you be home?" Annie asked.

"I'll be looking through these files. See you as soon as you can get here."

When Annie hung up, she told Brad about the records being in the Civil War materials and praised him for his sleuth work. "You were right, Brad. Of course, I want to go to Stephanie's and see what she's got, so as soon as I finish the laundry I think I'll drive over. Okay?"

"I'll finish the laundry. You go on over right now." Brad looked at the girls. "I'm sure you'll help me, won't you." A statement, not a question.

Stephanie hugged Annie when she arrived. "I'm so happy we found the records. I'm surprised Justin did all the work he did for Carter. And I can't figure out why he did. I haven't gotten through everything, though." She walked into Justin's office and pointed to the files she'd unearthed. "I'll keep going through this group while you look at the ones I've already seen. Maybe your eyes will catch things I didn't."

They both sat and paged through the records. Annie found Justin had set up a series of corporations for Carter, each one having a bank account in the Cayman Islands. As Annie thought about the corporations and their purpose, the only reason that made sense to her was to escape taxes, United States income taxes. She pointed this out to Stephanie. "I think Carter is trying to hide money he's made in real estate. I've heard people at Franklin talk about his buying and selling property. He'd have a lot of taxes to pay if that's true."

Stephanie was quiet but looked up from the papers in front of her as Annie talked. Then she said, "I've found a corporation that's in Justin's name and a bank account that's in my name."

"What?" Annie couldn't believe what she'd heard. "He's got a corporation attached to a bank account? And in your name? What's going on?" She got up to look at Stephanie's papers.

"There's got to be more to all this, Stephanie. I don't think we've found everything," Annie said after she'd looked at the new disclosures.

Stephanie was already going through more of the Civil War materials, searching for additional papers. She found them in the Gettysburg section of Justin's collection. A note prefaced a series of statements and Stephanie read it aloud.

Dear Steffie,

 If you've found these records, it means something's happened to me. I wanted to show them to you, but I was hoping to find a way out of the situation I got myself into and then I could forget all about the lapse of judgment I had.

 I started helping Carter Brislawn and his people with setting up corporations and bank accounts in the Cayman Islands because he said they'd pay me. So I did. It wasn't honest, but lots of people do it, I told myself, and pretty soon I realized I'd gotten myself into something I didn't want to be in. But it was too late. Carter wouldn't let me out of the deal and said he'd accuse me of changing some of the loan figures at Franklin and blame the fraud on me if I didn't keep on working with him and the others.

 Franklin people have blatantly been putting loans through the system that they've cooked the figures on. And I know Carter will make good on his threat if I quit helping him.

 I'm planning to talk to him early tomorrow morning at Sully's Restaurant and tell him again that I want out. I don't feel good about this meeting because I know he's very angry, but I'm hoping we can reach an understanding.

 I love you, Sweetheart.
 Justin

P. S. I recently put the Cayman Islands account in your name so you can get at our money.

ANNIE JUST looked at Stephanie when she finished reading what Justin had written to his wife. Finally Annie said, "I don't know what to think. It sounds like Justin was expecting Carter to do something terrible when they met. Do you think he anticipated Carter coming to your house?"

Stephanie shook her head. "No," she answered. "I think Justin was probably surprised to see him in the driveway. But he definitely was planning to meet with Carter early that morning. And he wrote his note to me before their meeting, perhaps the night before. I don't remember if he spent a lot of time in his study that night, but it wouldn't have been unusual."

Annie saw tears in Stephanie's eyes and felt a huge tug in her chest. How awful it must be for Stephanie, she thought, wondering if Justin was anticipating his death.

"Well, we have to go to the police with this evidence," Annie told her friend. "Justin was killed by Carter and we now know why."

But Stephanie shook her head. "Knowing why he was killed doesn't change the fact that I'd have to put Jose and Maria in jeopardy in order to prove what happened. I can't do that." She brushed tears from her eyes. "And I don't want the world to know that Justin was involved in tax cheating with Carter."

The empathetic tug in Annie's chest suddenly changed to an angry reaction. "Stephanie! We have to go to the police and Jose has to tell them what he saw! We can't let Carter get away with murder."

Stephanie didn't say anything, and Annie knew there wasn't anything that would convince Stephanie that Annie was right. At least not today.

Putting the files on the desk, Annie left the house without saying another word. It took all her willpower not to slam the door behind her.

Why had she spent so much time trying to discover Justin's killer when nothing would come of her time and effort? Why had she bothered to help Stephanie? It wasn't as if she had something to gain. Then she realized she'd tried to help Justin's wife because it was the right thing to do.

I'll find a way to convict Carter Brislawn III of killing Justin Diamond with or without Stephanie and Jose's help, she told herself as she got into her car and headed home.

CHAPTER 44

Confrontation was the only method Annie had thought of when she came to her office on Monday morning. She'd walk into Carter's office and tell him she knew he'd murdered Justin Diamond. He'd be surprised and confess, she told herself.

Being told that Carter wouldn't be in the office that day frustrated Annie. She'd spent the rest of the past weekend building up her courage and resolve to march into the president's office and deliver her accusations. Now she'd have to wait.

Sherm arrived and immediately asked her into his office.

"I've been on the phone with some of my contacts in New York. There's something big going on, Annie," he told her. "The feds are involved and there's been a lot of meetings with Wall Street investment firms. Lehman Brothers is going down and Merrill Lynch has been bought by Bank of America. In the past, every time there's been a crisis the heads of the biggest companies have united to work out problems. But my source says that this time it's every man for himself. He can feel the pressure, and he's not directly involved. It's all due to the subprime mortgage market."

Annie quickly responded, "But I don't understand. How could that cause such turmoil so suddenly?"

Sherm shook his head. "It goes way back, Annie. All those bad loans got packaged and sold to investors who probably didn't understand what they were buying. And now the default rates have gone way up. And the feds are worried."

"Should we be?"

"Probably. I don't know." Sherm shoved a file across his desk. "Nobody knows. My source says it could all have a domino effect because the investors and everyone else have so much debt."

"The old tulip story?" Annie asked, remembering her father's telling of the sudden fall of a tulip market in Holland that created a wholesale decline of an entire economy.

Sherm laughed, but there was a bitterness to the sound. "Yeah, kind of like that." He paused and then said, "I'm worried, Annie, worried about some of the people I've sold loans to. I don't know how deep this will go. My source is very alarmed and said 'Put on your seat belt, Sherm. We may be in for a real ride.'"

Annie was puzzled. "You think it could harm our home owners?"

"If companies get scared and can't get funding for their businesses, we could have a recession, people could lose jobs and then can't pay their mortgages. And if they're marginal borrowers?" Sherm coughed and Annie picked up the thought, "Or if they really didn't qualify to begin with?" she finished the sentence.

Sherm didn't say anything further and Annie didn't press him for further details. He'd already expressed his concerns.

She changed the subject. "Do you know anything about where Carter is today?"

"Probably out buying or selling houses. He does more of that than he does checking on the lending business he's president of." His voice had a critical, bitter tone. "I doubt he has any idea what's going on in New York."

Annie thought about confiding in Sherm and telling him about her evidence against Carter, and then decided to be silent. There wasn't anything Sherm could do about the situation, and, besides, Sherm was completely involved in his thoughts about the Wall Street crisis.

She'd talk to her dad about her meeting with Sherm.

By afternoon, however, the entire office was aware of what had happened in New York.

After she got home that day, Annie called her dad.

"Dad, are you aware of all the rumors going around about the big investment companies in New York City?" she asked him.

"You're not talking about Bear Stearns, are you? That was way back in March, old news now."

"No, Dad. I remember all of that when you told me Bear had been bailed out by regulators when the Federal Reserve got special financing to 'facilitate' an acquisition of the company. That's not what I'm talking about. Sherm told me it's a lot worse now and could lead to a real decline in *everything*. I'm thinking tulips, Dad."

Andy didn't laugh. "If Sherm says there's a big problem, I tend to believe there might be. He's got good sources."

Annie didn't ask her dad how he knew that. Her dad was always amazing her.

"I'll check into it myself," Andy said before he hung up the phone. "Your mother and I have been gone and haven't heard any news today."

Annie sighed. Whatever was happening was beyond her control, and even her input. She was glad she and Brad had controlled their debt and had consistently put money into savings.

CHAPTER 45

Looking haggard and drawn, Carter arrived at Franklin Mortgage on Tuesday morning. He told his secretary he wasn't to be disturbed, immediately closed the door to his office and reached for the telephone.

When he hung up after talking to the JWColbert New York office, he felt like the world had exploded and pieces of earth had landed full force on his aching head. *This can't be happening,* he said to himself after he'd been told that the company was at risk due to the huge amount of defaulting subprime loans they held. They needed a white knight to rescue them, a company who would buy them out, much like Merrill Lynch had been bought out by Bank of America. If the company couldn't negotiate a favorable sale, he was told, Franklin Mortgage would need to close its doors.

As his head throbbed, Carter felt he might be losing his mind. Everything had gone so well with his personal finances and he had made so much money that he'd failed to recognize the downturn in real estate and the danger of the fraudulent, risky loans he'd encouraged at Franklin.

He called his real estate broker and told him to sell everything in his portfolio.

"Are you sure?" Carter was asked. "The market's bound to go up again if you just wait out this slight glitch. Probably it's an excellent time to buy another property."

"Sell!" Carter yelled at him and slammed the phone down.

Leveraging his money had seemed like such a no-brainer when the market was heading up. Borrowing and using someone else's money had been the key to financial success. But now he was over his head, properties were going unrented, and his large income at Franklin Mortgage was in jeopardy.

"Slight glitch" was not the appropriate phrase in Carter's opinion. How had he missed the signs? He took no comfort in the fact that regulators had missed the warnings. Nor had the rating agencies who had given their seals of approval to the packaged, complex instruments. Even top management of many Wall Street companies had failed to adequately understand the risks they had taken. They were just like Carter, he now knew, and wanted the money the subprime loans provided.

He picked up the phone again but couldn't get through to his JWColbert allies. Angrily he jammed the phone on its cradle as though it was the telephone's fault that he was in a precarious financial position.

His secretary intercommed him to advise that Annie Robinson wanted to see him. "Tell her I'm busy and can't talk with her today. I'll try to see her tomorrow," he said. He had no intention to talking to Annie tomorrow, or the next day, or the day after that.

Sherm tried to gain access and was also denied. "I told you I didn't want to be disturbed." he yelled at his secretary when she called about Sherm.

Carter needed to think, to come up with a solution to his problems, to figure out what he was going to do if the company failed. He didn't have time for Franklin Mortgage employees.

If he took a big loss on his real estate, and if he had no income from Franklin, he realized he might need to declare bankruptcy. The money Justin had put through to his overseas accounts had been drawn out after the tax period for his sales had passed. Taxes had been the only reason for the accounts and the slew of corporations had provided a profitable shelter for his real estate gains.

"I won't end up broke," he said to himself. "There has to be a way around this." He reached for the phone to call New York again.

"ARE YOU sure Mr. Brislawn isn't available?" Annie had questioned his secretary. "I have to see him."

"I'm quite sure, Annie. And anyway it's not a good day to see him with the mood he's in," Carter's secretary had volunteered. "He snapped at me when he came in."

Annie's anger hadn't subsided since the weekend and, in fact, seemed to be growing with each day she couldn't lash out and accuse Carter. "So he's in his office?" she questioned testily. "And he won't see me?"

"Yes." His secretary seemed uncomfortable with the loan processor's continued presence.

"Well," Annie continued, "I can camp out right here as long as he can camp out in his office." She turned around and sat down in one of the leather chairs in the office.

Carter's secretary stared at Annie a minute and then resumed her work. Annie picked up a magazine on the little table next to her chair and flipped through the pages, feeling not even remotely interested in the business stories. She found the morning's edition of *The Wall Street Journal* and glanced at the front page. It was then that what Sherm had been talking about hit her, when she saw it in print. Lehman Brothers going down. Merrill Lynch being bought out. Voraciously she read the articles and editorials.

So, she thought, if these biggies can hit the fan, what about JWColbert? And what about Franklin Mortgage? Was this why Carter was too busy to see her?

Abruptly she put the newspaper down and got up. "I'll check with you later. Thanks," she said as she left Carter's office and headed down to her floor and cubicle.

CHAPTER 46

Wednesday came and went. Carter didn't contact Annie who grew more agitated each day.

Rumors circled wildly throughout the company as news of a possible sale of JWColbert spread. Would Franklin be sold? Would the offices close? No one thought this could possibly happen. But no one had thought Countrywide Lending would close. Annie just listened to all the talk. Work was slow.

On Thursday Annie positioned herself near the elevator on Carter's floor and waited for him to arrive.

When he did, he almost walked into Annie in his haste to cross the floor to his suite.

"What are you doing here?" he demanded harshly. "Are you going to tell me you've found something in someone's garbage? I don't have time to listen to your petty concerns. I have more urgent problems."

Annie didn't shrink from his glower and said, "I think you should take time to listen to me or you'll regret it. You think you've got problems now? Well, they're nothing compared to what they're going to be." She stared at him as hard as he was staring at her.

"What are you talking about?"

"Justin Diamond."

"What about Justin Diamond?"

Annie looked at his secretary's desk. "I doubt you'll want your secretary to hear what I have to say. Shall we go into your office?" and she pointed her head at his door.

An irritated Carter opened his office door and stepped inside. He motioned for Annie to follow him and then closed the door behind her.

"Now what is it you think I should hear?" he asked belligerently as he sat in his leather chair behind the desk.

Annie noticed Carter didn't invite her to sit down and seemed to think she should continue standing. Annie raised an eyebrow as she sat down in the chair opposite the president, looked him directly in the eye and without hesitation said, "I believe you murdered Justin Diamond in cold blood in front of his home. You shot him because he was trying to quit working for you on overseas banking accounts and forming corporations to avoid United States income taxes."

Annie saw color drain from Carter's face as she spoke, but when he answered it was to deny her accusation. "Oh, you can't believe such a wild story. Where in the world did you get such a preposterous tale?"

"You think I made it up? It might interest you to know we've found a witness." She felt as though she'd played a trump card by disclosing a witness to the killing.

But Carter's face showed no emotion. Just a lack of color. "I don't believe you," he said.

"You don't have to believe me. But it's true." Annie was surprised at her confidence. After waiting so many days for the opportunity to accuse Carter, she was glad to get it all said, to let Carter know she knew what he'd done. It was cathartic.

Carter bit his lip and said nothing for a moment. Then he answered, "So what is it you plan to do with this idiotic tale?"

"I plan to go to the police and tell them all about what happened, that Justin wasn't killed by a drive-by shooter. I just thought if you confessed to them, it would be better for you."

"Ha,ha,ha. You won't go to them. And you have no witness. And you have no proof. If you had, you wouldn't be sitting here now with me. All you have is your made-up story." Carter had relaxed as they talked. Color had come back to his face. He was back on his game.

"Now you need to leave my office because I have work to do. There's a real problem going on in this company, and the only thing you're doing is making the problem bigger," Carter told Annie. "Leave," he said again, this time more emphatically.

Annie was angrier than she'd been when she walked into the office. "You smug little worm!" she yelled at him as she got up from the chair. "You're a killer, and I know you shot Justin. You're not going to get away with it, not if I have anything to do with it!" She walked to the door, turned to Carter, and said "And, and I *quit*!"

She slammed the office door as she left, and Carter's secretary looked up from her paperwork with an amazed look on her face.

"Carter Brislawn III is a terrible person," Annie announced as she stalked from the room, her dark curls bouncing, ran to the elevator, and descended to the lower floor and her cubicle. *What have I just done*, she asked herself. She'd quit the job she had to have, all because she wanted justice done to Justin's killer. What would Brad say?

What would Sherm say? That was the immediate question because she had to tell him before she did anything else. His door was open, as it had been in times past before all his secretiveness had started, and she softly knocked on the hinge.

"Come on in, Annie," Sherm told her in his strong

baritone voice. "What's on your mind, besides the likely bankruptcy of JWColbert?"

Annie took a chair across from Sherm and said, "Actually, that hasn't been on my mind at all. What I wanted you to know is that I just told Carter that I quit." Annie felt drained of any emotion. All the build-up throughout the weekend and the beginning of the work week that gave her strength for the confrontation with Carter had evaporated, and she felt almost limp as she continued.

"I've been working with Stephanie Diamond to find out who shot Justin, and we discovered it was Carter. I confronted him and he denied everything, so I quit."

Sherm looked stunned. "What? You accused Carter to his face? What did he say?"

"He said I didn't have proof and had made everything up. Sherm, I didn't tell him about Stephanie, but I told him I had a witness, which is true, but he didn't believe me, or at least he said he didn't. I don't know. How can you tell with Carter? He has a face without muscles. No expression, unless it's anger, and I saw some of that."

Annie was starting to get her thoughts together, and her own anger returned. "He's such a, a *jerk.*"

When Sherm laughed, Annie relaxed a little more. "But I did quit, Sherm, and I don't plan to stay at Franklin Mortgage one moment more than I need to. I'll finish what I have on my desk and check out. I don't want to be associated in any way with a murderer." She rose from her chair.

Sherm was still in shock when he said, "You're sure Carter murdered Justin? How do you know that?"

"There's a witness we found," Annie said as she sat down again. "And we've found Justin's records of corporations and overseas accounts that Justin set up for

Carter to put his real estate profits in. And Justin left a letter for Stephanie that she just found in his Civil War collection. He wrote that he was meeting Carter the morning he was killed."

"So you've proven motive. What about the witness?"

"That's harder," Annie said almost bitterly. "A neighbor saw Carter and identified him, but it will be very difficult for the witness to go to the police. Carter doesn't know that. I was hoping he'd be afraid of the witness and he would confess. That didn't happen. And now he'll probably get away with the killing." She got up again, dejected at the thought.

"I don't know what I can do to help, but I'll try to think of something. I believe Carter is capable of doing something like you've described. In the meantime, I'd like you to change your mind, Annie. The word is that JWColbert hasn't had any success in finding a buyer, so they'll be selling all the assets they have, including Franklin Mortgage. And as you know, since we sell all the loans we produce, there won't be a huge value attached to the company, especially with the dark clouds looming over the value of the mortgages we've produced in the past. It's all a big mess." He coughed and then continued, "If you stay, though, at least you'd have a chance to get unemployment insurance. If you quit, you won't be eligible for it."

"I guess you're right, but I can't stay. I'd probably end up killing Carter." Annie smiled for the first time since entering the office. "And I probably wouldn't get away with it like Carter has."

She left the room, finished the more urgent files on her desk, and carried the remaining ones into Sherm's office. "There shouldn't be any problems with these. And I've made notes for Angela and you on all the files in process that are in my desk drawer."

"Please change your mind, Annie," Sherm pleaded.

"No, I don't think so. I've loved working for you, and if I ever get the chance to work for you at another company, I will. But not here."

She boxed up her personal items, said goodbye to a few people, and left the building.

WHEN BRAD came home, she told him what she'd said to Carter, including the phrase "I quit." Then she said, "And now I realize how much we needed my job, and I feel terrible."

Brad came over and hugged her, then kissed her on the forehead. "We'll be okay, honey. We can cut down here and there and we'll be okay. I'll bet you'll get a new job right away," he said confidently.

Annie shook her head. "If it's as bad as everyone seems to think, I doubt there'll be many jobs out there. And I'm so depressed, I'm not sure I'd be a good hire." She looked down. "And the thing that makes me feel the worst is that Carter will get away with murder. He'll go about his business of buying and selling houses, just as though nothing ever happened." She looked at Brad. "It isn't fair."

"How many times have you said 'fair' is what you take the kids to in the summertime. It has nothing to do with life," Brad said as he held and kissed his wife again.

Annie could no longer hold back the tears and cried on Brad's shoulder.

The next day, Friday, after she got the kids to school, she curled up on the sofa, turned the TV on, and scarcely moved all day. When the kids arrived home, she was still on the couch. Annie told herself she had so much to be grateful for, Brad, each of her children, her parents, their home, friends. She knew she had a good life. But she felt like a failure. She'd spent a year and a half trying to find out what had happened to a friend, Justin Diamond, and when she finally discovered who had murdered him, her life had come crashing down.

CHAPTER 47

Carter's head wouldn't stop aching. He took several more pain pills after Annie left his office.

Her accusation, coming on the heels of all the other difficult news of the past few days, had completely surprised him, and he'd been slow to respond. Once he'd caught a minute to think, however, he had quickly turned around the dialogue so he became the inquisitor and she became the defendant, a technique he'd learned in college and had found so useful in business. Catch your opponent off-guard, he'd been taught, and he had. Annie must have thought he'd just confess, and that wasn't going to happen.

Carter wondered how much of what she'd said was factual. Did Stephanie Diamond have Justin's records of their transactions? He had no way of knowing, but he suspected Annie was telling the truth. What he didn't believe was that she'd found a witness, someone who had seen him shoot Justin. It was early in the morning, no one was on the street, and no lights shone from any of the neighboring houses. She and whoever she was working with, probably Stephanie, had found no witness. It was only the records they had.

He needed to get those records.

AFTER BREAKFAST Saturday morning, Annie looked at the couch she'd spent the previous day on. What a wasted day, she thought, and reversed her lethargy by attacking the kitchen cupboards with all the energy she could muster, removing the items, washing the shelves, cleaning the contents, and then re-arranging them as she'd intended to do for months. Rachel wasn't thrilled to help, but was conscripted for the job. Once she got into the work, she seemed to enjoy the conversation between herself and her mother as they worked together on the task.

Rachel talked and Annie listened to her daughter's tales of faithful girlfriends, unfaithful boyfriends, and fathomless teachers who couldn't seem to tell the difference between students who did their own work and students who cheated. It was therapeutic to Annie to realize that nothing really changed in the world, and the world kept going from one generation to another. Progress was made an inch at a time when it came to handling our feelings and our concern for justice.

When they had finished, Annie thanked Rachel who smiled and said, "It really wasn't so bad doing all this work, Mom."

Annie felt happy that she'd taken the time to hear her daughter. She realized in the months before she hadn't spent enough time doing that.

Gage asked if he could take Taffy for a walk and stop by his friend's house.

"Yes, but make sure it's okay with his mother for you to have the dog there."

"Oh, they have dogs. It'll be fine."

"But *ask*, Gage," Annie told him.

She called Stephanie and told her about her meeting with Carter and that she'd quit her job.

"Oh, I'm *so* sorry, Annie," Stephanie told her. "I never intended for you to lose your job because you were helping me."

"I was helping bring justice to the world, Stephanie. And I'm not giving up."

"But what can we do?" Stephanie sounded as depressed as Annie had been the previous day.

"I don't know, but I'm not giving up."

Cammie and Candy had been invited to spend the weekend with Linda and Andy and had happily packed their small backpacks with all the items they thought they'd need, including their electronic games since Grandma and Grandpa didn't have any of them in their house.

Linda had told Annie, "Having the twins will be fun and will give you some time off."

Annie was grateful, but she missed the hubbub the twins always seemed to carry around with them.

Gage called and said he and Taffy had been invited to have dinner and spend the night with his friend. "Are you sure Taffy's also invited?" Annie questioned.

"Of course. They like Taffy."

"Well, okay, then."

Rachel asked to spend the night with a friend.

It seemed as though there was a conspiracy to make the Robinson household very, very quiet that evening.

Annie curled up next to Brad as they watched a movie on television and promptly fell asleep.

ALL THE pain pills Carter swallowed didn't make his headache better. Instead, it kept getting worse. He had to think, had to figure a way to keep Annie from going to the police with the records Justin had kept.

Friday was a terrible day with news from JWColbert that the company was filing for bankruptcy. In addition, at about four o'clock he got a call from his real estate agent that it would take more time than he had expected to unload the properties and get cash.

After getting Annie's address from company records and learning everything he could about her family, he left the office early, with merely a cursory look at his secretary.

With his view of Elliot Bay from his condo that evening, he watched the ships as he self-medicated with Scotch, then smoked the hash he had. He imagined himself on a cruise ship in the Mediterranean, an arm around a dark-haired beautiful woman who looked much like Rita. The ships continued to pass by his large penthouse window, but he no longer saw them. A hazy sleep had come over him.

When the phone rang the next morning, he reached to answer it and then saw it was his mother calling and put the receiver down. He hadn't talked with either of his parents for several months, and this definitely wasn't a good time to remedy that omission.

Groggy, hungry, but still with a headache, he ambled to the kitchen Saturday morning, reached into the refrigerator for tomato juice, and slogged his way back to the couch. As he slowly drank his juice, bit by bit he started creating a solution to his Annie problem and could see the pieces coming together.

After finishing his juice, he cooked a large breakfast of three scrambled eggs, fried potatoes from a frozen package, four pieces of toast, and strawberry jam. Strong coffee completed the meal.

The headache continued and he took more pills.

He dressed in jeans and a shirt and drove his Porsche from the condominium garage into the light traffic and headed out of downtown.

Surveillance was the key to a solution, he told himself. And he could be very patient.

CHAPTER 48

Gage Robinson wasn't having a good time at his friend's home. For one thing, he worried about his dog, Taffy, who didn't seem welcome by his friend's two dogs who kept shoving him away from where they were playing with Gage and his friend. For another thing, he didn't like the food they were going to have, meatloaf. Annie always made him a hamburger patty when she fixed meatloaf for the family, but Gage didn't feel comfortable saying anything. The third reason he wasn't having a good time was that he didn't want to be away from home at night; he wanted his own bed with Taffy at the foot on top of the covers.

Late afternoon he told his friend's mother that he would walk home with Taffy. He thanked her and said he appreciated the invitation to dinner, but he thought he should go home. No, she didn't need to call his parents. He would be fine with Taffy.

A white Porsche slowly started down the street as Gage and Taffy made their way home. As the Porsche pulled up alongside the boy and his dog, Taffy tugged at the leash like he was impatient at their pace. Carter leaned across the passenger seat, lowered the window, and asked, "Is that you, Gage? I'm your mom's boss. Could I give you and your dog a ride?"

Gage hesitated. How often had he been told not to get into a stranger's car? This directive had been drilled into him and his sisters repeatedly. But surely it would be all right for him to ride with his mother's employer. And it would be fun to ride in a Porsche.

"What about my dog?" he asked.

"He can ride, too. Get in and I'll drive both of you home."

Gage continued to hesitate and Carter got out of the car. He walked around the rear and opened the car door for Gage as he said, "It's nice to meet you, Gage. Your mother is one of my favorite employees. Here, let me take the leash while you get in."

Gage climbed in and Carter slammed the door, letting go of Taffy's leash as he did. A startled Gage tried to get out but Carter locked the door, raced to the driver's side and was sitting next to the boy before Gage could react. "But my dog!" Gage yelled.

"Your dog will find his way home, Gage, but you and I are going for a drive," Carter angrily replied as he tied the boy's hands and put a blindfold over his eyes. "Now just sit quiet and you'll be okay."

Carter pulled the Porsche onto the street as Taffy barked and ran after the departing car.

Twenty minutes later they pulled into the driveway of one of the unrented homes Carter owned. As Carter led the still handcuffed and blindfolded Gage into the house, he said, "Now we'll see how much your mother loves you."

WHEN ANNIE awoke Sunday morning, the first thing she was aware of was the sound of scratching and a dog whining. She turned over in the bed and said to Brad, "Do you hear a dog?"

His reply was muffled and he covered up his head beneath the covers.

Annie got up, reached for her robe in the closet, then shuffled to the front door in her furry slippers. When she opened the door to see what was making the scratching sound and Taffy came bounding in dragging his leash, she let out a scream. "Taffy, what are you doing here? Where's Gage?" she asked the dog and received a tail wagging answer from an obviously weary animal.

"Brad!" she yelled. "Something's happened with Gage. Taffy's here." She took the leash off Taffy and went to the phone to call Gage's friend.

Before she could call, though, the phone rang. Thinking it was Gage calling, she said, "What happened? Taffy's here. Is everything okay?"

In a voice Annie immediately recognized, Carter said, "Why yes, it is. I thought an early-morning call would be good, just to let you know Gage is doing fine, just fine. Would you like to talk to him?" and he handed the phone to her son.

"Mom? Mom? I'm okay, Mom. But I want to come home. Please come and get me."

Carter grabbed the phone from Gage and said, "Yes, your boy wants to come home, and I want him to also. But it's up to you, my dear Annie. It's all up to you."

"What do you want me to do?" Annie asked with a trembling voice. "I'll do anything you want."

Brad came into the living room, a questioning look on his face. "What's going on?" he asked.

With her hand Annie motioned to him to be silent.

"Good," Carter replied. "Then I think we'll have a deal. I want you to bring Justin's records of our transactions to me. Is it his wife you've been working with? Stephanie, I believe her name is."

"Yes," Annie softly replied.

"Stephanie, that's right, that's what Justin called his wife. He said she's beautiful, as I recall." Carter didn't speak for a moment and then continued as if there'd been no lapse, "And that he was a lucky man. He wanted to be able to buy her nice things. Yes, that's what he said."

Carter's voice sounded strange to Annie. Was he going mad? Was he crazy enough to harm Gage? She was close to being sick. "I'll try to get the records. Where are you?" she asked.

"Try is not a good word to use, Annie. You're to *get* the records. Comprendo?"

"Yes, I understand. I'll get the records. Where do I take them?"

"That's much better, Annie. Bring them back to your house and I'll contact you there. Tell Stephanie, that's who has them, right? Tell her you and your husband need to look at them and that you're just borrowing them." Carter's voice still sounded different to Annie.

"How do I know Gage won't be hurt?"

"I guess you'll just have to take my word for it. Of course, it's your only hope of getting him back. And do I need to tell you not to contact the police? I don't think so. You're a smart woman and that would be very, very stupid." Then he said, "And when I meet you, I want your husband with you."

Carter hung up.

Brad caught Annie just when she started to fall. He brought her to a chair and got water. "Drink this," he said as he handed it to her. "And then tell me what that was all about."

Annie related the entire story and then said, "Brad, his voice didn't sound right. I'm so scared for Gage. Carter killed one person, and I'm afraid he'll kill our Gage." For the second time that weekend, Annie burst into tears.

As he had the night before, Brad hugged his wife, and then said, "I know how hard it is, honey, because he's our son and we're both scared." He kissed Annie and then continued, "But we have to get to Stephanie's house right away. I don't want Carter to think we're not doing what he wants."

Annie blew her nose and sat a moment longer, drinking the water Brad had brought, then they quickly dressed and drove to Stephanie's house.

"What if she isn't up?" Annie questioned as she rang the doorbell. "It's Sunday morning."

But a surprised Stephanie answered the door and got the records when Annie asked her for them. "We're thinking we might get another lead if Brad goes through them. You don't mind, do you? We'll get them back soon."

Stephanie handed the boxed records to Brad. "Good luck," she said. "I can't imagine your finding anything Annie and I haven't, but you men think alike."

Annie and Brad looked at each other. "Yeah," Annie replied, "they sure do."

Any other time Annie and Brad would have had a laugh over Stephanie's comment, but not today. Today they didn't even smile.

CHAPTER 49

Carter had taken the blindfold off Gage's eyes the night before when they got to his rental home. He kept his hands tied, though, and told him he wasn't to talk. After tying Gage's feet so he couldn't walk, Carter had left for a brief time and brought back a milkshake for Gage and a steak sandwich for himself. They slept in sleeping bags.

"It's just like camping, isn't it, Gage? Have you ever camped with your dad? My dad never took me camping, but I got to go one time with a friend and his dad. It was a lot of fun. We had a tent and sleeping bags, and we roasted hot dogs. I remember looking up at the stars and putting sticks with marshmallows over the fire. Did you ever do that?" He looked at Gage for a response and Gage nodded his head.

"Yes, I'll bet you did. All kids do that with their dad. Except me. My dad built boats, Gage, beautiful boats. Have you ever been on a boat?" Again, he looked at Gage for a response.

"No," Gage answered with a trembling voice.

"That's a shame, Gage. Boats are a lot of fun. I really like boats, but my dad just built them. He didn't have much time to go out on the water in one." Gage watched as Carter got up, put something from a bottle in his mouth, and swallowed it with a glass of water. "Do you want some water, Gage?"

Gage nodded his head yes and was handed a glass.

"How did your folks come up with your name, Gage? It's a good name and I like to say it. Gage, Gage, Gage," he repeated. "I'm named for my father who was named for his father, so there are three Carter Brislawns. I think it's a good name, don't you?"

Again Gage nodded his head. But this time his eyelids closed.

"Oh, so you're sleepy, Gage? Well, you just settle down and get some rest. Tomorrow we'll talk to your mother," Carter said more to himself than to Gage. "We'll all have a good visit and see if your folks can help me solve a big problem."

He continued muttering to himself before he also fell asleep.

The following morning Carter awoke early and began pacing the floor. When Gage stirred, Carter again tied his feet and left briefly, bringing back coffee and two egg sandwiches and a soft drink.

"Now I'll untie your hands so you can eat," he said to Gage as he handed him a sandwich and drink, "but keep your feet tied so you can't get away. I remember how fast I could run when I was your age." He took several bites of his sandwich and drank much of his coffee. "I never had a soft drink for breakfast. How about you? Do your folks let you have soft drinks for breakfast?" he asked as he looked at the child. He didn't seem to expect an answer and continued eating and drinking.

Not having eaten for hours, Gage finished his sandwich with only a few bites and drank his drink with two long gulps. He stared at Carter and waited.

Suddenly Carter looked at his watch and made a phone call to his real estate broker, slamming the phone down when he heard nothing had transpired in the past 24 hours.

Then he made another phone call, this time to Annie.

Following the call, he untied Gage's feet, blindfolded him, and said, "Get up. We're going to see your folks," and he shoved Gage out the door and into the Porsche.

They drove the short distance to Annie's house where Carter watched Annie and Brad leave, then followed them at a distance to Stephanie's home. In his mind's eye, he saw Justin standing in the driveway and flinched slightly as his ears replayed the shots fired that early morning. He saw Stephanie come to the door, go back in, and then return with files in her hand. She handed them to Brad.

He watched Annie and Brad drive back to their home. Then, again from a distance, he called them.

"I WANT to talk to Gage," Annie said after the phone rang. She knew it was Carter. "I need to know he's okay."

"He's doing just fine, but here, I'll let you talk to him," and Carter handed the phone to Annie's son.

"Are you okay, honey?" Annie asked, fright in her voice.

"Yeah, Mom, I'm okay. But I'm scared and want to come home."

Carter grabbed the phone and looked at Gage. "Why did you say you're scared? Haven't we had a good time? Didn't we have a good campout last night? Didn't I feed you great food, even pop at breakfast?"

Gage nodded his head.

"You had a good time, didn't you?" Carter asked again.

"Yeah, I had a good time," Gage answered obediently.

"That's better. You always agree with what adults say. It's what kids are supposed to do." He didn't realize Annie had heard the conversation and said to her, "Gage is doing very well, Annie. I think he's enjoyed the time we've spent together. He's a great kid. Maybe we can go camping together again."

Brad took the phone from Annie, whose face was turning white. "What do you want us to do, Carter. We got the files you wanted," he said.

"Well, hello, Brad. You have a great kid, and we've had a good time together. I was just telling Annie I'd like to go camping with him again," Carter responded.

"You wanted Justin's files and we got them. Now you get our son to us!"

"There's no need to get angry, Brad. You sounded like my dad when you told me what I was to do, and I didn't like that, no, not at all." Carter rubbed his forehead as he talked. "Let's see, where did I want to meet you? Oh, I remember. I want you and Annie to drive to the office. I'll be out in front of the building with Gage. Bring the files, of course."

Brad heard the phone click.

NEITHER ANNIE nor Brad noticed the Porsche following them from a distance as they drove the familiar route to Franklin Mortgage. Not a word was said as they tried to think everything was going to be all right and they'd soon have their Gage back with them.

They pulled into the deserted parking lot, quickly climbed out of the car and walked to the front of the building. Traffic fronted the office, but on Sunday it was lighter than other days and buses ran less frequently.

Carter drove to the lot from a side street. He got Gage out of the Porsche and hustled him to the front of the office building, standing behind him as he addressed Annie and Brad from 20 feet. He grasped Gage's arm and then removed the blindfold. "Well, here's your boy. Where are the files?"

Brad held them out to Carter. "Now let Gage go," he said.

"I told you I didn't like to be told what to do, and you keep telling me what to do. Are you stupid or something, is that what you are?" Carter was yelling and waving his free arm.

"I'm sorry, I didn't mean to tell you anything. I just want my son back."

"There's a couple details I need to check on first. Annie said there was a witness. That's not true, is it?"

Both Annie and Brad shook their heads.

"I didn't think so," Carter said, laughing as he talked. "And you don't intend to tell anyone about any of this?"

Annie and Brad both shook their heads again.

"How about you, Gage? You're not going to tell anyone, are you?"

"No, no, I won't tell anyone," Gage excitedly said. "Not anyone ever, ever."

"Okay, Gage. Walk over to your dad and get the files, then bring them to me." He pulled a gun from his pocket. "And please don't try something silly. It would be easy to shoot your mother."

Gage looked at his captor and then ran to Brad, who extended the files to him. He ran back to Carter, hands outstretched to him.

In Annie's mind, time stretched out as she watched and waited for Carter to let Gage come to them. Would he keep his word and release her son?

Carter was waving the gun as he talked. "You have a good boy in Gage. I like him," he said in a loud voice. "I don't suppose you'll believe me, but I felt bad when I shot Justin. We had worked well together until he started telling me what to do and what not to do. He just wouldn't listen to me, and the only thing I could do was to shoot him. You understand, don't you, Annie?" he questioned. "Everything was going well." He rubbed his forehead. "Now everything's not going well. It's not going well at all. I tried to be a good president of Franklin. Didn't you think I was a good president, Annie?" he asked.

Annie nodded her head and said, "You were an excellent president, Mr. Brislawn. The company made a lot of money."

"Yes, a lot of money. And now JWColbert's going to declare bankruptcy and it's all going to be gone. Everything." He continued to rub his forehead. "And my houses are going to be gone...." He looked at Gage. "You're a fine boy, Gage," he said and then looked into the street before again turning his gaze on the young boy. "I wish you had been my son. We would have gone camping together, maybe fishing." He gently released Gage, pausing slightly as he did, glanced at Annie, dropped the gun on the sidewalk, and stepped into the street as a bus passed.

Annie screamed and both Annie and Brad raced to Gage's side. Papers flew out from Carter's hands as the bus screeched to a sudden stop. Carter lay on the pavement just past the front tires that had run over him.

Annie and Brad ran to retrieve the scattered papers and Gage ran to the man who had kidnapped him, sobbing as he did.

"He was so mixed up and unhappy," the confused youngster said as his parents reached him and put their arms around him. "He kept telling me how much he liked me. I didn't want him to die."

With her arms around her young son, Annie said, "Of course you didn't. None of us did."

Chapter 50

The police came, but not before Annie and Brad had a chance to prepare Gage for their questioning. "As far as we're concerned, Gage," Annie told him, "we were merely meeting Mr. Brislawn because he wanted to convince me to return to Franklin Mortgage. We don't want to say anything about your being kidnapped or anyone being killed. Mr. Brislawn was a very troubled person. You could tell that. I can't see that anything would be gained by telling the police anything more. Do you agree?"

Gage nodded his head in understanding.

Brad said, "We'll all talk further when we get home, son."

When the police had talked with them and said they could return home, Gage climbed into his parents' car and commented, "I'm going to buy a Porsche when I grow up."

Relieved the ordeal was over and their son was safe, Annie and Brad smiled. "I have dibbs on the first ride," Annie told her son.

"I dibbs on the second," Brad chimed in.

Annie couldn't quit being happy on the way home.

RACHEL WAS told what had happened, but all agreed not to say anything to the twins, who were still with their grandparents.

"I can't believe you went through all you did, little brother. I'm so proud of you," Rachel told Gage as he continued to put his arms around Taffy.

"I did something bad, though," Gage said apologetically. "I got in a car with someone I didn't know, and I knew better than to do that. Mom and Dad always told me not to. But when he said he was Mom's boss, I just thought it would be okay. And the Porsche was so cool."

Annie felt so much love in her heart for her son.

"Why did he kidnap me, Mom? I hadn't done anything to him. Why would he do that?"

Gage was striving to make sense of something that made no sense to any of them, but Annie tried to explain. "He wanted lots of money, honey, and did some awful things to get it. He kidnapped you to hide one of the terrible things he did, killing someone. There's no excuse. There really isn't." Annie reached over to kiss her son. "But sometimes adults do things they know better than to do, things their parents told them not to do, or if not their parents, then society. And adults decide what they think is 'cool' and often make unwise choices to get what's 'cool.' As you get older, you'll be making choices, and I think you'll make good ones. It's okay to think a Porsche is cool and to want to own one, Gage. It's perfectly okay if that's your choice. But it's how you go about getting it that's important."

Gage was still perplexed. "He didn't talk right, Mom. He kept telling me about his dad and not going camping with him, and a whole bunch of other things. And he kept taking some pills, for a headache he said. In a way, I felt sorry for him."

He petted his dog, "I'm so glad you're okay, Taffy. I was so worried about you."

Annie knew this would always be a special moment in her life.

Linda and Gary brought the twins home, and the room was again a chaotic, noisy place, much to Annie's pleasure. "Chaos is good," she whispered to Brad.

"I missed you, Cammie. You, too, Candy," Gage told the girls as they spread out their dolls and all the doll clothes they'd assembled. "I'm glad you're back home."

They looked at their brother as though he'd said something quite strange and unbelievable. "He's gotten all weird," Cammie told her sister.

"Home is good, Mom and Dad," Gage told them. "It's wonderful."

WHEN THE four children were in bed, Annie and Brad sat next to each other on the couch and talked about their concern over not telling the police the real reason they were at Franklin Mortgage that day.

"I don't want Gage to think he doesn't have to tell the truth to the police if he doesn't feel like it," Annie told her husband. "Have we done something we'll be sorry about?"

"I honestly don't know, honey. When Carter stepped out in front of the bus, it was such a shock that my only thought was to get Gage away from there and home."

"Me, too. I didn't want to be there a moment longer. I kept looking at Gage's face, and all I wanted to do was grab him and leave."

They sat a moment and neither spoke. Then Annie said, "Now I know how Jose must have felt when he saw Justin shot. Conflicted, for sure. His life would have completely changed and the risk would have been so great for him and his family if he had gone to the police, but he felt bad that he hadn't told the truth. It bothered him so much that he told Stephanie."

Brad nodded his head. His arm was around Annie who continued talking.

"If we'd talked with the police, though, we would have had to explain just why Carter had kidnapped Gage, and that would have led to the records Stephanie gave us, and that would have led to my accusing Carter of murdering Justin, and that would have led to there being a witness, and that would have led to Justin's part in the dishonesty, and that would have...." There was a muffled sound as Brad kissed his wife.

CHAPTER 51

Following school on Monday afternoon Annie returned the records to Stephanie, who had read about Carter's death in the paper that morning. "It's over, Stephanie, and no one will ever know about Justin's part in Carter's life, and Jose won't need to worry about testifying to what he saw. You can do whatever you want with these records," she said as she handed them to the widow. "I think Carter acted alone and there weren't others involved. I think he told Justin there were others just to frighten him."

Stephanie appeared relieved to hear Annie's feeling that Carter acted alone. "I really didn't know if I'd get the records back, Annie. You seemed so insistent about getting them Sunday that I wondered if you'd decided to turn them over to the police," Stephanie responded hesitantly.

"Really? It never occurred to me to give them to the police." She had planned to tell Stephanie about the kidnapping but suddenly decided to keep that piece of information to herself. "Anyway, our problem's solved. Carter's death put an end to it," she said and turned to go.

Stephanie put her hand on Annie's arm. "Thank you, friend. You helped get me through a terrible time in my life, and I'll always be grateful," she said.

When Annie left, she wondered what Stephanie would do about the money in the overseas account Justin had put in her name. Would she get the money out of the account and back into a United States account? Or would she leave it there forever? Annie didn't care. In Annie's mind that morning, it was none of her business. Her business was her family, her children, her husband, and that was just fine with her. She'd never wanted an overseas bank account. She just wanted all her family to be safe.

FRANKLIN MORTGAGE was in turmoil Monday morning after Carter's death.

Sherm called Annie to see how she was. Having no idea of Annie's part in Carter's life-and-death decision, he commented, "The newspaper said you and Brad were there because Carter wanted you to come back to the office. Did you accuse him of murder?" he asked. "What did you say to him?" Then he paused before asking, "Would you come back now?"

Annie laughed. "I've been out of the rat race for two work days, and it's really felt good not to have the pressure."

"Yeah, I can imagine," Sherm replied. "But I've been thinking of something I want to run past you. Can we meet for lunch tomorrow?"

Glad that Sherm hadn't pressed her harder about her accusing Carter of murder, Annie hesitated. She didn't know what Sherm had in mind, but she knew she needed some time off. Lunch would probably be fine, though. "Sure. Where?"

They set a time and place.

Annie reached the restaurant before Sherm and was ordering coffee when he arrived. "I'll have coffee also," he said.

Annie stirred her coffee even though she hadn't put either cream or sugar in it and sat quietly as Sherm began the conversation.

"How's Gage doing? The paper said he was with you and Brad when Carter died. Pretty tough for a kid to witness," Sherm said as he watched Annie closely.

"He's doing well. Thanks for asking. We talked a lot about it last night and I think that helped," Annie replied.

"And how about you?"

"I'm enjoying the time off. I hadn't realized how many hours I spent thinking about our borrowers even when I wasn't at the office."

They both ordered sandwiches and Sherm continued talking. "We've officially heard that JWColbert is going into bankruptcy and they're trying to sell the remains of Franklin Mortgage. The exit door hasn't shut since the word came down to us."

"What are your plans?" Annie knew this was the reason Sherm had asked her to lunch, and she was curious what he wanted to do.

Sherm took a bite of sandwich and a sip of coffee. "Well, I'm very much wanting to open a branch office for another lender I've been talking to. I think the economy is going to be very difficult for quite awhile." He took another bite and said, "I'm hoping you won't go to work for someone else right away, and that you'll work as my loan processor again when I get started. I won't be able to offer you what Franklin did, of course, but I think we can make a go of it. What do you think?" He put his sandwich down on the plate as he looked at her.

Annie didn't know what to say. She wasn't sure Sherm had really learned his lesson about the fraud he'd been involved in. The only way to find out was to ask him, she decided. "I'm afraid you'll get desperate enough to start changing documents, Sherm. Have you truly learned?" She returned his direct look.

Without a moment's hesitation, Sherm answered, "Yes."

Then she asked, "And what about Angela? Will she be coming to work for you?"

"Never." The emphasis in his tone was hard to miss.

"You're a good loan officer, Sherm." Annie let the silence dwell over the table for a few minutes as she thought about Sherm's plans and his offer. He didn't press her for an answer, but she decided to give him one.

"I don't want to start work right away, but if you want me when you open your new business and I have about a month off, I'd like to work for you. I doubt I'd be able to train another guy as well as you've worked out," she told him.

Sherm laughed at her. "That's great, Annie," he said. His voice sounded relieved.

They moved on to other subjects, and Annie asked about Melanie and his children. "How are they all doing?"

"Better, I think. Lance seems to be working hard at school." He didn't say anything about Lance's drug problems and hoped he would never need to tell her. The possibility of Lance's relapse hung over both Sherm and Lance, but so far Lance was successfully battling his demons.

"And Melanie isn't drinking. For her, it's one day at a time. I'm home more now," he continued.

"You were gone from the office so much for awhile. Drumming up business, I always assumed." Annie was enjoying her sandwich as the conversation moved from Sherm's offer.

"Yes." The answer needed amplification, but Sherm furnished none.

Annie looked at him questioningly but didn't say anything.

There's something he's not telling me, she thought. But in the same way she'd decided the overseas bank account was Stephanie's business and not hers, she decided that whatever secret Sherm had was his business. It wasn't hers.

Justin's murder had been *her* business until she'd figured out who had shot him and why he'd been shot. She wouldn't share that with Sherm because there was no reason to tell him. Both Justin and Carter were dead and had died violently. Hopefully, that would be the end of violence in her life.

They talked about all the fallout on Wall Street and what any bailout would mean. Sherm commented, "I doubt any of the heads of companies will pay for the mess they had such a big part in. They'll skate."

"I've read that their companies are too big to fail. What do you think about that?" Annie asked.

Sherm slowly shook his head. "I don't think it's that the banking companies are too big to fail. I think it's that they and their officers are too powerful to have to account for what they do. I hope I'm wrong. Sometimes I think I know more than I want to know about this industry," he said quietly.

As Annie listened to Sherm Taylor, she was already starting to get excited about a new job.

CHAPTER 52

Sherm followed the Franklin Mortgage ship as it went down, declining to submit his resignation immediately, contacting as many of his clients as he could to tell them of the bankruptcy of JWCollert and the imminent closing of Franklin. He completed loans that were within underwriting guidelines of the company and pressured the escrow companies to get signings and funding as rapidly as possible. He did everything he could to maintain faith of the borrowers.

When the doors finally closed, he was one of the few employees who hadn't gone through them to find other employment.

His visits to see Rebecca had dwindled in late summer and fall and finally on a Portland trip in October he discussed his confused thoughts with her as they sat next to each other on her couch. "I don't know what to do. I love you, Rebecca, but I can't leave Melanie right now. She's been doing so well, and she depends on me."

Rebecca didn't respond to his words immediately. She looked at him, then looked down at her hands before bringing her right hand up to rub the back of his neck, and said, "It's okay, Sherm. I understand. You never told me you didn't love Melanie, and I've known how you felt about responsibility. It's okay."

Sherm felt he was letting down the person in his life that meant the most to him, but he knew he couldn't leave Melanie.

The return drive to Seattle was emotionally painful after he and Rebecca said goodbye. He knew he'd made the right decision, but he couldn't overcome his feelings of regret. Maybe in time he would.

No amount of time would ease his regret over the fraudulent actions he'd taken, though. He wondered how he'd been so convinced he was doing the right thing to change documents. When had he started crossing the line between honesty and dishonesty? And when had he ceased to even *see* the line?

Having so much to do to get his new branch office formed kept his mind occupied the following month. Unfavorable publicity had accompanied the closing of Franklin Mortgage and he put several advertisements in the newspaper to announce his new office, hoping to attract qualified buyers who didn't know where to turn to get a housing loan. It was a slow slog, but gradually his fortunes improved.

When he opened his office, true to her word, Annie came to work for him.

"I can't believe I missed the pressure," she told him.

"I can," he replied.

THE HOUSE Annie and Brad found had been marked down like a fire sale item. The Seattle economy had tanked much like the rest of the nation and it was a buyer's market which Annie and Brad took advantage of. Annie processed their loan through Sherm's new company and, of course, all the underwriting guidelines were followed. A large down payment was applied. Underwriting had no problem approving it.

Annie asked the twins if they minded once again sharing a room. They looked at her much as they'd looked at Gage when he said he was glad they were home. "Okay," Annie told them, "so I'm weird for asking."

Rachel hadn't wanted to move so far from her friends, but she quickly found new ones who also had cell phones. As a reward for all her help with Cammie and Candy, Annie and Brad upgraded her cell phone and increased her allowance.

Gage had the most trouble with the move and Annie wondered if it was due to his horrible kidnapping experience that made him want to stay in a familiar area. Brad spent more time with him and found a soccer team Gage liked. "His adjustment is just going to take more time, honey," Brad told his wife.

As long as Gage was with him and he could sleep on top of his bed, Taffy was happy wherever he was.

Annie loved the house. It would be a good home for her family. The wait was worth it.

CHAPTER 53

In January, 2009, on the two-year anniversary of Justin Diamond's murder, Annie left work early, stopped at a floral shop where she purchased a small bouquet, and drove to the cemetery. She wasn't surprised to see a large floral arrangement placed at the gravesite by Stephanie.

As she looked at the etching on the stone, she thought about what it didn't say. Does a gravestone etching ever say anything about death by murder? She asked herself. Only in Old West cemeteries where the violence is displayed as "shot dead," or "hanged on yonder tree."

Justin's grave should have a marker reading, "Justin Diamond, shot by Carter Brislawn III, who also kidnapped Gage Robinson and got away with it." Except Carter really hadn't gotten away with it, Annie decided as she looked at Justin's marker. Carter hadn't gotten away with much of anything, although he'd not been arrested for mortgage fraud, tax cheating, murder or kidnapping. His ramblings had shown him to be a delusional individual living a warped life, a man who must have felt he had nothing left to live for when he took his last step into the street fronting his once-powerful position.

Annie put the flowers on Justin's silent grave and looked once more at the gray stone etched with Justin Diamond's name, date of birth, and date of death. "Bookends," she murmured. "Like bookends, we put birth and death dates on a marker. In between those dates we put nothing, nothing about a person's life, nothing about who they were, although it's a person's life and who they were that we remember."

Annie thought about Justin's smile, their friendly conversations, his confidence in her, and his loving letter to Stephanie.

"Justin, your killer is dead, Stephanie is well, and no one will ever know your part in Carter's scheme. I hope you will rest in peace," she said softly.

Annie slowly returned to her car, sat quietly for a few minutes, turned the key, and drove home to her family.

Tomorrow would be a busy day at the office.

ABOUT THE AUTHOR

Helen Christine was born in Caldwell, Idaho, and graduated with a B.A. from The College of Idaho in Caldwell. In the years between school and retirement she taught school, worked in financial services, and was a business owner.

Along the way Helen gathered material for novels—plots, characters, and the twists and turns of both—and following retirement restarted the writing process begun in school in Caldwell.

Helen enjoys listening to music, reading fiction and non-fiction books, watching movies and favorite sports teams, playing bridge with patient people, chatting with grandchildren, and spending time with family and friends. Helen and her kitty now live in Spokane, Washington.

Printed in Great Britain
by Amazon